Robert's writing skilfu p the nature of life's big qu e you read, and understand then these stories are highly
PAUL KERENSA - COMEDIA

These stories are certainly very thought-provoking. I found myself empathising with many of the people and situations in them...We all struggle to deal with our demons, so read on, you are sure to identify with some of the big questions contained in this book, and perhaps even find some answers.
CHRISTINE WRIGHT - COMMERCIAL PROOF READER

A fantastic collection of engaging short stories which pose refreshing, intelligent questions about the big issues such as life and death; purpose and existence; beauty and ugliness; truth and lies.
JENNY BUTTER - EPIPHANY LIFE COACHING

I have to say that I found the stories both gripping and moving... I recognised some of the depths that several of Robert's characters experienced in the stories, and the way in which he described these depths rang true, as did the way in which they struggled with the big questions of life and meaning. He brings out the importance of the big philosophical questions for everyday living and, in doing so, he makes them so much more accessible than the reading of a philosophical textbook could.
JOHN SHORTT, PROFESSORIAL FELLOWSHIP IN CHRISTIAN EDUCATION, LIVERPOOL HOPE UNIVERSITY.

Some of these stories are really powerful and I'm taking much longer reading them than I thought I would. I would not hesitate to send them to my mates, or even the lads at work.
QUIGGERS - PRISON OFFICER

CW01619923

The author manages to introduce deep questions without slapping the reader in the face with them. Enticing the reader with an intriguing story and then relating the struggles of the characters to our day to day thoughts.

Dominic Benstead - RAF pilot

The individual stories contained in this book have the potential to engage the reader and provide an opportunity for a spiritual health check across a broad spectrum of topics. They might help provide clarity on ones current direction of travel, or perhaps offer an alternative perspective as an aid to decision making. The various chapters will help the reader to probe a little deeper into some of the fundamental issues, exposing areas that need to be addressed, as a means to enhancing ones quality of life and wellbeing. Furthermore, the independent nature of the bite-sized chapters mean that this book is perfect for picking up and putting down, as time allows.

Angela Hamilton

NHS Associate Director

Head of Patient Experience, Public Engagement, and Spiritual Healthcare

Random Lives

Thoughts on life and Eternity

By Robert Jackson

Copyright © 2018 Robert Jackson
This edition published in April 2018.

All Rights Reserved worldwide under the Berne Convention. No portion of this book may be reproduced, stored in any information storage and retrieval system or transmitted in any form or by any means—whether electronic or mechanical, now known or hereafter invented—except for brief quotations in reviews, without the prior written permission of the author.

This is a work of fiction. Names, characters, places, and incidents either are the product of the author's imagination or are used fictitiously, and any resemblance to actual persons, living or dead, events, or locales is entirely coincidental.

An edited version of *Descartes in a Car* was recently published by Hymns Ancient and Modern Ltd, and this full version appears with their kind consent.

Published by Clanucy, Shetland, United Kingdom.

Author: Robert Jackson
Design: Michael Watermeyer (mwatermeyer.com)

Cover image used under license from Shutterstock.com:
copyright © 2018 Rawpixel.com/Shutterstock.com.

ISBN: 978-1-9996514-0-4

To my friend and brother,
John Williams,
who saw me through.
A Psalm One Man.

Contents

PREFACE

First Things First

"The unexamined life is not worth living"

— Socrates —

Some years ago, I visited Stonehenge. This justifiably world renowned set of boulders lies in a field next to a stretch of road in southern England now known as the A303. Gazing at the giant stones brought to mind an earlier visit that I had made a significant number of years before. Being only six or seven years old at the time, I could remember virtually nothing about it, and that I would claim to have been with my family is based on shrewd deduction rather than clear recall. In fact, the only thing I was able to recall was a memory stimulated by the fence that was now preventing me from walking up to and touching the boulders themselves, something that I clearly remember doing four decades earlier. My other memory associated with the place was reading the Ladybird book about it. In it, we were taken through a plausible explanation of how the stones were hewn from mountains in Wales, transported to Salisbury Plain, and raised into position. One wonders whether, in the near future, a bunch of energetic students, led by an inspirational lecturer (and doubtless accompanied by a keen BBC film crew) will try to recreate this amazing feat of our ancestors.

Interestingly, no-one has ever suggested that Stonehenge is a naturally occurring phenomenon of nature. That geometric formations of regularly shaped rocks occur in nature is a fact—visit Fingle's Cave on Staffa. That stones of a certain type crop up some distance from their source is a reasonably common feature of land that has experienced glaciers—they're known as *glacial erratics*. And as for precariously balanced boulders, again, this is not unknown in the natural world. So, why is it that we unthinkingly assume Stonehenge was created by humans? Beyond the unlikely combination of all these features in one location is the fact that the boulders also appear to have been carefully aligned to mark an event synonymous with June the 21st—the rising of the mid-Summer sun. Frankly, the chances of Stonehenge being a naturally occurring phenomenon are so small as to be effectively non-existent.

Lingering just beneath the surface of the monument itself, however, is a far deeper mystery. There arises a question—one that neither the Ladybird book, nor, for that matter, any other book on the site that I am aware of, even acknowledges. And, despite the fact that Archeology has exposed so many of the secrets of Stonehenge, this particular question pertains to a different branch of scientific study altogether. The mystery is this: how is it that atoms, molecules, stuff—call it what you will—gathered into one particular formation, can be manipulated by a collection of pretty much the same sort of atoms and molecules originating from the same lifeless planet, simply because they are arranged in a different way?

We could put it another way. If you and I were to head back to the beginning of everything, we would be informed by those who have studied such matters that there were initially only two elements in existence—Hydrogen and Helium. Today, experience tells us that somehow, these two elements morphed into many other elements, which in turn linked up to create complex molecules. These then combined to form not only inanimate objects like boulders, but living objects, such as plants, animals (sentient objects), and, amazingly, reasoning objects (humans). It is worth noting here that in recounting this, I am trusting the testimony of others—I have no idea whatsoever how one can possibly carry out the research that leads to these conclusions. Most scientists, though, seem to be confident of their facts, even if there is a small but vocal number of them who are prepared to offer an alternative account.

You see, unlike with Stonehenge, there is no unanimity as to the origins and purpose of humans. So, just what is this blob of flesh that is, properly speaking, what all of us are? If one so desires, one can study Physiology and cut up dead bodies in order to work out our constituent parts in chemical terms. On the other hand, TV documentaries mean that you don't have to have a degree in Physiology to recognise what an amazing thing the human body is.

When your father ejaculated inside your mother's vagina, he released enough sperm to fertilise pretty much all the women in Europe. Therefore, to contemplate one's origins as a random encounter between just one of these tiny sperm and your mother's minuscule egg, and then to compare this encounter with what you see in a mirror, is properly mind-blowing. And in those more profound moments in front of a mirror—when we peer deeply into our own eyes and ask 'who is this person?'—our material composition is the last thing we're thinking about.

When it comes to Stonehenge, most people simply see a remarkable testimony to the unexpected ability of our ancestors, but, for a few, it is so much more. It is the place where they can honour the rising sun and tune into the spiritual forces of Earth's very own life-giving star. They wish to do this because they have a particular worldview that is relatively uncommon in the United Kingdom. The fact that they are so few in number means that they are cheerfully, if somewhat condescendingly, tolerated. People don't, as a rule, fall out over interpretations of Stonehenge.

This is not always the case when it comes to interpreting human life because some worldviews play a far more significant role in the understanding of our origins. Currently, in the West there is a fairly aggressive battle raging between various life philosophies. For the sake of convenience, I shall divide these into two categories based on their approach to one defining feature, namely God. One group believes that there is a God (or Gods), and the other believes that there is not a god (or gods). Unfortunately, those who would place themselves into the second category often trivialise the question of God's existence. Some liken it to the question of whether there is a flying spaghetti monster[1]. The reason why this is unfortunate

1. In 2005, Bobby Henderson wrote an open letter to the Kansas State Board of Education demanding that if intelligent design was to be taught in schools, then his theory that a flying spaghetti monster created everything ought also to be taught. In due course, the Church of the Flying Spaghetti Monster was established in New York and *Pastafarianism* was born.

is because the fact (or not) of a flying spaghetti monster has very little bearing on the question of human existence and purpose. On the other hand, the question of whether or not there is a God who is ultimately responsible for the Cosmos clearly does have an enormous bearing on how we view ourselves, the Cosmos, and the small matter of the purpose of life.

Now, the fact that I am an ordained priest in the Church of England testifies to the fact that I have a *Theistic* world view. In other words, I look at the world through the eyes of someone who accepts that God is. I believe that God created the Cosmos from nothing, and I could go on and write out a statement of faith, but, in the interests of brevity, I'll stop there. Yes, you might argue that I have a bias, but, in reality, this bias is no more than the influence of my worldview on the way in which I interpret my experiences. C.S. Lewis had a really neat way of putting it when he said:

> *"I believe in Christianity as I believe that the Sun has risen—not only because I see it, but because by it, I see everything else."* [2]

In exactly the same way, those who have a worldview that excludes the existence of God interpret their experiences in the light of this belief, and so exercise exactly the same kind of bias that I do.

What am I getting at here?

There are many who would argue that unless I leave God out of my work, then my views and opinions are biased, and therefore of limited value. This strikes me as a rather irrational

---

2. This comes from *Is Theology Poetry?*—a paper Lewis delivered at Oxford University's Socratic Society in 1945

demand since it assumes that my Theistic worldview is less valid than a Materialist[3] one—a claim that cannot for one second be demonstrated. Sadly, many people have been persuaded that this is the case…that the Materialist worldview is somehow neutral because it deals only with facts that can be demonstrated scientifically. As a result of this, any notion that God is the God of history is strictly banned from the classroom, and the 'why' questions that so often occur in science lessons have to be answered from an atheist perspective. The Darwinian account of natural selection is not allowed to be challenged. Please note that this so-called 'neutrality' doesn't require the materialist to compromise any aspect of his worldview, whereas the Christian has to abandon the very heart of hers. It is hard to see why this exclusive approach can in any way be described as 'neutral'.

Writing in 1922, Bertrand Russell couldn't work out why China lagged so far behind Europe when it came to science. Why did all their Alchemy never become Chemistry? Russell was a purveyor of the Atheist misrepresentation of the Church's relationship with Science. He wrote:

> *"Although Chinese civilisation has hitherto been deficient in science, it never contained anything hostile to science, and therefore the spread of scientific knowledge encounters no such obstacles as the Church put in its way in Europe."*[4]

---

3. Materialism argues that only physical matter exists and if it doesn't show up in a laboratory, then it can't exist. Clearly, God and spirits and souls etc. fall into the 'can't exist' category.
4. Bertrand Russell, *The Problem of China*, George Allen & Unwin, London, 1922, p. 193.

As a school chaplain, I discovered at first hand the success of the Atheist agenda in science lessons. The 'neutral' presentation of science resulted in pretty much every fifteen year old I encountered instinctively denying that one can be both a scientist and a person of faith. To counter this, I created a series of lessons that looked at the relationship between Christianity and Science. I wanted the pupils to understand that of all the world's religions, it was Christianity's belief in a God who is rational that led to the application of reason to the observed world. In reality, it was not the Church as such, but rather the Establishment that resented its authority being challenged by the subsequent scientific discoveries. Far from being the impediment to progress, as Christianity is regularly portrayed, it was in fact its very incubator—not least since all the early scientists were themselves Christians.[5]

One day, a group of pupils came up to me and said it would be cool if I could arrange a debate between a Christian and a Scientist. I went one better and invited Simon Conway Morris, a Christian and a Scientist who has occupied the Chair[6] of Evolutionary Palaeobiology in the Earth Sciences Department of Cambridge University since 1995. His work on the Burgess Shale fossils and the resulting scientific concept, the Cambrian Explosion, has been ground breaking. He has forged a theory of evolutionary convergence in which humans are an inevitable consequence of an evolutionary process that bears no evidence of the randomness demanded by Materialists—the very

5. If you want to know more about this, read Rodney Stark's book, *The Victory of Reason* published by Random House in 2005.
6. He's a professor!

randomness that becomes necessary when removing the need for a Creator. Whilst the Materialists challenge his work, it is nevertheless the product of scientific research. Whilst his research is widely taught, his carefully argued interpretations are, in the interests of so-called neutrality, largely ignored.

The school's Head of Science at the time was a Materialist, and I got the distinct impression that he was not thrilled at my inviting Simon to come and speak. Happily though, he agreed that, with such an eminent scientist coming to the school the lecture should be made compulsory for his pupils. This meant that for once in their school lives, they heard an understanding of evolution that included the 'God' word…quite a few times actually. At the end of the day, the science of Evolutionary Palaeobiology is all about digging up fossils, studying them closely, and combining this with all manner of research conducted on living creatures. The interpretation of this science is another matter, and all I did was ensure that the pupils were offered an equally viable and, as far as a Cambridge University Professor is concerned, more plausible alternative to the Materialist interpretation.[7]

So, I invite the reader to tolerate my worldview and to read on. You are about to be offered a number of short works of fiction. Whilst each of them is a story in its own right, I have attempted to order them in a manner that reflects the development of Western thought. I hope that they will all be interesting with each doing

---

7. If you're interested, Francis Crick, one of the first discoverers of human DNA, was a Materialist, and Francis Collins, who led the international team that finally completed the map of the genome, converted from Materialism to Christianity in his late twenties. Two Francis's, two interpretations, one science!

more than merely occupying half an hour of your time. Some might detect a Philosophical thrust, and maybe there is one. But I tend to feel uneasy about labels because I think they stifle creativity by generating expectations through the establishment of often arbitrary boundaries. That being said, what follows is aimed at a readership that knows enough about this sort of thing to want to know more.

The material arises out of 14 years of teaching at my last two schools where I was confronted by small groups of 17 and 18 year olds who were on the brink of adulthood. I decided that it was my duty to make sure that, before they left school, they had been introduced to the big questions of life, the *mirror questions*. By *mirror questions*, I mean those you ask of yourself when looking in the mirror—especially at those times when you are feeling a little uneasy about life. They are really important because the answers you arrive at will have a big influence on the way you live your life. At the same time, you look in the mirror with frustration, because you can never be absolutely certain of the answers—of which there are usually several conflicting ones for each question. Questions like 'Who am I?' or 'What is the purpose of my life?' or 'What happens to me when I die?' or even 'Is there a God?' My contention is that these *mirror questions* are also religious questions since all religions have to offer answers to them. Indeed, any worldview that proffers such answers is, in this sense, a religion.

Now, I will be trying to get to the heart of what a few really influential people thought—some of them as long ago as 2,500 years. I know more about some than others, and a number I know only in as much as I have read what others, who have studied them, have said. For instance, there's a Dane called Soren Kierkegaard who had some important original thoughts back in the 19th Century. He wrote quite a lot of books, and I did buy one and start to read it…several times. I'm afraid it did my head in trying to work out what he was saying. I think I was probably like a Grade 3 double bass player trying to understand a full orchestral score. A lack of technical knowledge, however, has never prevented me from enjoying such music, or from being introduced to its nuances by those who do have the insight. I am really pleased, therefore, that people do study Kierkegaard. (I have this theory, though, that if you get to the point where you can understand in depth what he was on about, you might have lost touch with the way in which a 17 year old mind operates —something that I reckon my nineteen years of teaching has given me a fair insight into.) So, I like to see myself as working in partnership with those who dig deep into the thoughts of the wise sages of the past. It's a bit like forestry work.

There are some who understand trees at a very deep level. They understand their molecular structure, their growth patterns, their relationship to other plant and animal species, their vulnerability to parasites, and so on. Their knowledge is invaluable to the estate manager who has to look after not just the trees, but the rest of the estate with its economic concerns. So, if you were to ask me about Kierkegaard's contribution to Western thought in terms of his existential ideas, I could help you. And, if you wanted a detailed analysis of his work, then I could also help you…by pointing you in the direction of someone who has the knowledge. But be warned. A recent peer-reviewed article by an Australian named M.G. Jacoby, claims that Kierkegaard wasn't an existentialist in the first place, and that he only toyed with the idea.[8] Whether or not he was—and who will ever know for certain—is not as important as the idea of existentialism itself.

So you might disagree with some of my takes on the thoughts of the philosophers who crop up in the stories. So be it. Kierkegaard wrote in Danish, a language I don't understand [9], under different pseudonyms in order to present different points of view. Even the journals that he handed to his brother before his death seem to have been written in such a way as to deliberately conceal what his true thoughts were. Indeed, it would not surprise me if he never actually knew precisely what his thoughts were in the first place. If so, what chance do I have of getting him right? In a sense, it really doesn't matter if what I've said about, say, Plato is accurate or not, because there can never be a definitive version of his philosophical ideas. Not only that, but if he is a deeply thinking human being, it is highly likely that his opinions and views were being constantly tweaked in response to his experiences. His body of work, known as *Plato's Republic*, might well present a view that could have changed after he wrote it. What does matter is that in setting out his understanding of life at a point in time, he provides as many questions as he does answers. And I guess that this is what my stories are really about, in that they flow from my imagination, and reflect my understanding.

---

8. See *Kierkegaard on Truth* – Religious Studies 38,27-44.
9. Translating complex works always involves interpretation…and this goes for the sacred texts as well. This is why the Koran is only the Koran if it is in its original Arabic and if you want to read it, you have to learn Arabic.

Whilst you are, of course, at liberty to disagree with my influence through the stories I tell—indeed, the stories might even annoy you—I do hope (and pray) that you will engage with them. Be warned though, for if you find yourself accusing me of deliberately twisting information as a means of supporting my Christian worldview, there is a chance that you're not honestly facing up to the challenge that these stories might have offered up to your worldview. I believe that, in order to grow, mature, and become WISE, you need to take your views and opinions into places where they will be challenged and allow them so to be. This takes a certain amount of humility and involves a fair degree of risk—there are a number of well-known figures from history who appear to have completely messed up their lives by thinking too hard for too long. Hume offers a great lesson here. As you will read, the renowned Scottish sceptic opened the door to a form of Nihilism, but it would appear that, whenever he found himself drifting towards the door, he invited his friends round, opened some bottles of port, fished the backgammon boards out of the cupboard, and got on with living.

I hope you will be stimulated by what follows. All I'm trying to do is help you to see that the questions of life have been swirling round for at least as long as people have been able to record their thoughts for others to share. I suspect that you will find that what our forebears came up with will often resonate with your own thoughts and experiences. And perhaps you will recognise how they have left their mark on the society in which you and I live today. Most of all though, I pray that the stories will be used by the Living, Loving, Creator God who is at the heart of my worldview, to creatively interrupt you as you journey along the once-only road that is your life.

"The unexamined life is not worth living"

— Socrates —

Dolphins

"The purpose of life is to pursue happiness during our life. A good life is a happy and exciting life. The ultimate measure of life's success is the happiness in our life."

— Principle No.6, The Secular Humanist, Purpose-Of-Life blogspot —

Hannah breathed in deeply and bobbed beneath the surface of the water for what was probably the twentieth time this session. She was getting tired, and so the length of time she could spend sharing the world of the dolphins was now down to around ten seconds. This would be her last dive. Unlike the previous sessions, however, she was not stopping because she was tired. On the contrary, it was because she was finding that, instead of simply enjoying the company of these puzzling creatures, she was beginning to get angry. It had not always been thus.

On the first day, with the help of Nate, the therapist, she had entered the dolphins' pool without a moment's hesitation. Somehow, they had drawn her in and made her feel welcome as a guest in their world. From the very outset, they had given her a real sense of worth. How, she wasn't sure, but they seemed to have a way with her that said she mattered. By the end of the first day, she found herself able to kick with her fins and swim underwater in their company for maybe thirty seconds at a time —but always, as she well knew, this was only because they were prepared to accommodate her.

Back at the hotel that first evening, where she was staying with her parents, Hannah had been her customary uncommunicative self. Her parents were disappointed that their gentle probing was not acknowledged. Whilst this was nothing new, they had hoped that, after what they had witnessed of Hannah with the dolphins, she might have said something.

Nick and Helen had been allowed to watch the afternoon session from a discreet vantage point. At first, Nick had found himself reflecting on the fact that her swimming costume revealed that his daughter was now very much a woman. Had he noticed her growing up? Had he properly involved himself in her life? He honestly didn't know. Huge amounts of his time were eaten up by his gruelling career as a GP—something for which he was perfectly capable of berating himself. At least, however, he had usually been able to leave his work at the surgery, and keep his weekends largely free. Helen, his wife, had been the one who had taken on much of the burden of raising the girls. Though he had always been around to discuss child-rearing issues, it had been easier to let her get on with it...girls together and all that. Whilst he had kind of wanted a son, he had found himself more than content with daughters, and at any rate, a third child had not been possible. That Helen had survived the birth of their second daughter, Martha, was a minor miracle in itself. The loss of her womb, and the consequent removal of any chance of a male heir, had been a small price to pay.

He looked at Hannah across the table in the hotel dining

room and though she was not responding, Nick sensed that her silence wasn't the deliberate sleight it normally was. She was simply lost in her own private world. He switched his attention to Helen. The past eighteen months had not been easy on either of them, but somehow, Helen had found it harder to cope. Nick had found it far from easy but he had a bloke-ish ability to compartmentalise his life so that he appeared less chewed up than in reality he was. All this had contributed to a deterioration of a marriage that he had been so utterly certain of. Nick was in a very uncomfortable place. Did Helen feel the same way? Perhaps he was a coward for not broaching the subject with her. He knew it was crazy not to, but he sort of hoped that perhaps Helen might think things between them were still ok—that it was just him feeling this way. In any case, to burden her with the issue of their marriage, on top of the past events, would have been cruel in the extreme. He knew deep down though that this was not the case.

But this afternoon, watching Hannah in the pool, they had experienced a moment that was so deeply shared between them that Nick found ground to believe that he might be mistaken, that they might not be treading a diverging path after all. It was as though something had swept away the messy clutter of their life together and they had held each other and wept.

Helen had started it.

She was in a very dark place indeed. Whilst in her head she believed that there must be a light flickering somewhere, her battered heart prevented her from looking for it in case it didn't exist. She had arrived at a point where she could no longer picture what a liveable life might look like. Having vainly explored a number of possible destinations, she found she no longer had any sense of direction. This trip to Florida was a pathetic attempt to create a destination—it had given her something to plan, to arrange, to organise. Only when she was doing these things was she in control, and to be in control was what she craved more than anything. It was the only way she knew of mollifying the distress she experienced in the face of uncertainty.

The past year and more of Hannah had presented her with uncertainty by the bucket load. Instinctively, she had tried to take control, to work out the solution, and to guide her family towards it. When one solution failed, she found another and so the process was repeated. Nick's suggestions hadn't worked either, and his inability to help—combined with the fact that he was able calmly to head off to work each morning—annoyed her in a way she knew was irrational. Witnessing Hannah's misery and deepening depression had been hard enough, but this manic pursuit of a solution had essentially shattered the mother/daughter bond that had been so much a part of the joy of raising her. This remoteness from Hannah seemed to have induced in her a sense of isolation—a disposition which only served to push Nick away at a time when she desperately needed his quiet solidity. Ironically, it was precisely this solidity that she found herself resenting. How could he return from work each evening and chat on about the same patients whose aching throats and grumbling guts were so often little more than an excuse to sit in the company of the one man who was prepared to listen to them. *Nick was far too nice...to his fucking patients. What about me?*

The word fuck had become a common word in her silent vocabulary, and indeed it was starting to venture into her spoken one. Helen didn't know what she thought about this. Because it was so out of character, she liked the fact that it expressed—to those who knew her—the strain she was under without her having to tell them. It had even slipped out during a conversation after the morning service on the Sunday before they had flown out to the States. Her close friend, Jo, had simply been listening to her and offering words of love and support. When she had promised to pray for the Florida venture, Helen had suddenly and unexpectedly let fly. God had done nothing to help Hannah to date—he hadn't helped her to love Nick, he hadn't mended her heart, and he hadn't looked after Martha. Jo's carefully worded undertaking to pray had been angrily rebutted…"Don't bother Jo, it's been fuck-all use to date!" Afterwards, she admitted to herself that this had probably been a deliberate gesture to Jo, a friend whose faith and love had become a little too perfect for comfort.

All this had played on her mind as she and Nick had been led to the vantage point that overlooked the dolphins—was Jo praying right now? Could her prayers do any good? Did God exist beyond her deeply conditioned imagination, and where was Martha at this precise moment?

Anyway, as she looked down at the massive concrete tank, she saw several objects swirling around beneath the water and it was a few seconds before one of the smaller ones broke the surface. She immediately recognised her daughter, and then watched as a second human head surfaced, followed by the grey shining head of a dolphin. She searched Hannah's face for a reaction, and then it happened. Helen was transported by a wave that swept her away to a place she had not known for many dark months. She literally wobbled as her legs began to buckle beneath her, and a lightness entered her soul that was bursting bright. She grabbed for Nick who was standing beside her, and his presence was as solid as ever. But this time, rather than feeling condescending, it was once again reassuring. She felt his arms wrap themselves around her and she relaxed into his strength. He held her carefully for it was imperative for both of them to be able to keep their eyes on the most fabulous sight imaginable. Hannah's eyes were bright, and her mouth was split into a grin of almighty proportions. As far as they could tell, her whole body started to convulse as the sound of the laughter reached the embracing couple.

Before she knew what was happening, Helen was in tears, and Nick, unable to help himself, was sobbing with a physical intensity that he was completely unaware of. Together, as one, they were witnessing a Hannah that they had not seen for more than a year—a Hannah they feared had died with her sister. It was as wonderful as it had been unexpected. Yes, this is what they had hoped and prayed for. But for Nick, a GP, dolphin therapy was also 'Quackville Daytona' that you naturally had to travel to the US for. If all the very best efforts of the NHS had left Hannah unaffected, what the three bells could a couple of bottle-nosed dolphins achieve?

If Nick's medical sensitivities had been assaulted, Helen's default pessimism had also taken a hit. Even though this whole trip had been her doing, she had been assiduously preparing herself for the inevitable let down. She had reckoned that if she was prepared for it then it would hurt less, though in practice, this was rarely the case. Anyway, she had been chatting with Rebecca, one of Nick's partners, who had casually mentioned dolphin therapy. Rebecca was the practice partner whose dress code revealed a conscientious refusal to subject herself to the diktat of the fashion houses. She went annually to the Glastonbury Festival as a volunteer helper, and she had a decidedly open mind when it came to alternative (wacky) initiatives in medicine. Drifting, as she did, towards a syncretistic version of earthy, Eastern spirituality, she understood the body to be more than a physical entity to be treated with a range of chemicals. Helen liked Rebecca. She liked her ability to resist the pressure to conform, and although she was always ready to consider different approaches to medicine, she was actually a bloody good doctor. Her feet, in spite of appearances, were firmly rooted to the ground. (Oh, and she had a fab kitchen.) Helen was also just a little jealous of Rebecca's ability to ignore what others thought of her. It wasn't that she wanted to be like her, far from it, but there was something deliciously attractive about her devil may care attitude. So Helen had read the article proffered by Rebecca, googled 'dolphin therapy', and had made a decision. It was worth pursuing. Not only would it assuage her feeling of helplessness, but she would have some potential panacea to pursue—and this particular one would be a challenge.

Nick had baulked at the idea for two reasons. First, he was a GP with a sense of dignity, and secondly, a week's therapy cost $2100—and this was before flights and accommodation. Helen had been determined though, and Nick, having sounded out Rebecca's thoughts on the matter, had decided to go along with it. He, like his wife, was desperate for a way out of the blackness of Hannah's depression. Conventional drugs, counselling, and persistent prayer had all, as yet, failed. It would also give his wife a possible solution to work on, and at that particular moment, this was probably more important to him than the remote chance that dolphin therapy might have an impact on his daughter.

And so there they were, husband and wife, hugging each other in a way they had not done for months.

Hannah was oblivious to their presence. This first time with the dolphins had quite simply blown her away in a manner that she could not possibly have foreseen. The morning passed in consultation with the American therapists had not filled her with optimism. This in itself was hardly surprising since even the word optimism had become meaningless; it referred to a concept that she could no longer relate to. Why had she agreed to this latest in a line of often embarrassing attempts on the part of her parents to help her? Probably because, somewhere deep inside, she still clung to the notion that she loved her parents —notwithstanding how she might feel about them most of the time. This theoretical love had become the only constant in her life, and whilst it regularly teetered on the edge of the precipice, it had yet to topple over. Of late, she had taken to looking from her mother's abdomen, which once enclosed a womb, to her father's crotch, and imagining the moment of insemination that had brought her into being. Bizarre that such a trivial act could create her in all her complexity. The adolescent revulsion she had always felt at the thought of her parents 'doing it' had been replaced by a fascination at the link between the act and her own identity. She had read about sex, and well over half of the girls in her class had slept with boys. Hannah, though, could no longer separate contemplations of sex from images of Martha. It had become a no-go area, save for her baffled musings that tried to work out how the mystery of life could have such a banal genesis.

She had, from the moment of learning of Martha's death, taken to looking at herself naked in the mirror. She wanted to see if she could tell who she really was. What made her her? Why wasn't she Martha? Why was Martha not any more, and yet she, Hannah, was? How could you be no more? It was a bizarre notion; that which is so real, so me, can in fact be terminated. Yet, how could all this go on without a me to observe it? She would narrow her eyes and try to penetrate their reflection as she sought out her identity, her real self, stripped bare of the lies she lived—lies that projected to others, and to herself, the image of the person she wanted to be. All had become entirely fatuous. She didn't want to pretend anymore. She wanted to be herself in an authentic manner, but what on earth did this mean? Martha had been a person just like her, and she had been close to her younger sister. How could she ever move on?

Martha's death had been her fault. She had persuaded her parents that they should let her go to the party because she was fourteen. Hannah had, at the time, been on the top of her form. She had asked her parents to deny the fact that they had gone to similar parties at people's houses when they were fourteen, and she had seen her mum acknowledge the force of this. Martha had been desperate to go because she had just taken up with Nick (how weird to have a boyfriend with the same name as your Dad), who was in Hannah's year. He was in fact a nice lad, and although he moved outside of her own circle of friends, she was pleased for her sister. She had told her Dad that Nick was a straightforward, pleasant boy and that if it was this age gap that was the problem, hadn't he, at sixteen, also gone out with a fourteen year old? Hannah had triumphed on behalf of her little sister and the party was on!

Martha had simply disappeared from the party.

One moment she had been there, and the next she had gone. Nick—the boyfriend—hadn't looked for her because he had been really mad at her. He had hoped Martha would have been more compliant with a bit of drink inside her, but even after a couple of ciders, she hadn't allowed him to get past first post. His hand had been snaking its way up her skirt, and an awkward scene had ensued when she had fought it off.

Embarrassed, Nick had yelled, "You frigid bitch!"

Martha had stood up, swung around and stormed out, her face mottled with tears and mascara. No one saw her again.

One of Hannah's more painful acts of self-abuse was to recall, in detail, her Mum and Dad sitting behind a table that had a range of mics clustered on it, their black cables contrasting sharply with a white cloth. A policeman in a smartly pressed uniform sat in the centre, his hair carefully brushed over a balding forehead. To his left were Mum and Dad, and to his right a couple of other people—she hadn't noticed them at the time because all she could see was Mum, helplessly convulsed in tears, and Dad trying to read a script whilst just about holding it together. She had remembered watching such scenes on TV with Dad. He would generally mutter something about a sad voyeuristic population being fed tragic titbits by an amoral media greedy for ratings. The police had persuaded him that their distress might persuade Martha, who in all likelihood had run away, to return home. If in fact something more final had occurred, then again it might persuade someone with pertinent information to come forward. The pain of watching Dad feed such voyeurism had been unbearable at the time, and the passing of the months hadn't diminished it.

That evening, Martha's body was found in an industrial wheely bin round the back of Morrison's supermarket. She had been beaten, raped, and strangled. Martha had fought for her life, and the police had found bits of flesh under her finger nails. The release of this information had caused a woman to report a work colleague. She had always found him aggressively macho, and abhorred his attitude towards women which she described as bestial—on a good day. She had been curious about some gouged scratches on his face and what the policeman had said on TV offered a plausible explanation as to their origins. The forensic precision of DNA testing did the rest.

As the finality of Martha's death gradually became a reality in her life, so Hannah's guilt became acute to the point where she convinced herself that she, and not the killer, was responsible. She found herself full of self-loathing for those times when she realised she was not experiencing the pain of guilt. She needed the pain. She needed to feel the full weight of a punishment that could never be allowed to end; only an eternal punishment had any chance of being fit for the crime she had committed. It was obvious that her parents were making a supreme effort not to appear to blame her, but she knew that they, along with everyone else, knew precisely who was at fault. And she had felt so smug at the time of presenting her compelling case, the case that had sent Martha to her death.

The dolphins didn't blame her. They bore no grudge against her. She knew that they must sense her evil nature, just as everyone she encountered clearly did. But, unlike people, they welcomed her, smiled at her, and swam alongside her. One of them had looked into her eyes and there had been a connection that expressed an unconditional acceptance of this stranger into their world. It was absolutely their world, but they allowed her to express herself—they accommodated themselves to her awkwardness, and they swam at her speed. It was amazing.

She also remembered the evening of that first day when she had sat at the meal table. Yes, she was aware of her parents' questions, but she had been completely preoccupied, contemplating the possibility that a living being could actually think she was lovely. It was an amazing but unsettling thought. Where did that leave the eternal punishment that she was duly enduring? So she had retreated behind her silent veneer once again, and once again, she felt the exposed hatred of her parents towards her. Ever since Martha's death, they had been trying to cure her, not for her sake, but because they wanted to get their happy family back. She was fed up with them abusing her in this way, and this trip to Florida had, in her mind, been the last straw. Why had she agreed to co-operate? Crazy as it sounds, she had decided that there was no way she was going to go to tacky Florida. Then…she found herself watching one of those infernal nature documentaries. One wants to be tired of them, but if you start to watch, they almost invariably suck you in—animals are fun to observe, even the human ones. Anyway, this particular Sunday night (she had long since stopped going to the church youth group, and her parents had stopped caring about that as well), it was all about a group of dolphins. They had developed a way of chasing stingrays out of thick seaweed so they could feed on them, but what captivated her was the woman who was swimming with them. Not only did she know the individual dolphins by name, but she seemed to be known personally by them. Swimming with dolphins looked cool, and if her parents were wanting to take her to Florida to swim with them, she would oblige. This would, however, definitely be the last time she would allow them to push her around. She would have to work out a way of coping with her mother's selfish schemes, and it might even be that the time was coming to cast herself adrift and leave home.

Helen lay in bed. It was their third night in this American hotel room where the beds were extravagantly huge, exactly the same as everything else in the States. Two double beds in a large room counted as a 'twin', and she and Nick had not even discussed the possibility of treating them as anything other than singles. They had slept apart on the first night. After their emotional hug the day before, they had shared a bed, and each other, for the first time in months. Tonight, it had been a little more awkward. They had wanted, both of them, to recreate the experience of the previous night when everything had just happened. The pressure to recreate, though, brought to the fore the fact that they had been drifting apart for so long that, in spite of some pretty deep chats during the day, they were still some way away from being the couple they had been. Sex had been clumsy and a million miles from the previous night, but at least they were in the same bed. But Nick was asleep and, in spite of herself, she allowed it to annoy her. Sleep always seemed to come so easily to him. She did, however, enjoy his warmth, and as she lay there, she let her mind wander. Normally, she was pretty self-controlled about where she allowed her thoughts to go because she knew where she might end up. Perhaps it was Nick's reassuring presence that caused her to lower her guard and she found herself imagining Martha, and wondering where she was. Obviously, this would end in acute pain, but now that she had started, she couldn't stop. Yes, Martha was dead, but where was the bright young thing that she had borne and nurtured for fourteen years. Could it be that death had ended her? Was she simply as a match that was once lit, had burned for a while, and had then been snuffed out by an unexpected breath of wind and disposed of. End of match—end of Martha. The molecules that formed Martha were never anything more than a random arrangement of atoms that combined to give the chimera of a person. Even as she had lain in her coffin, these same molecules had started to disperse as the flesh rotted. Maybe some of them would end up in a tree that, in due course, would be processed into matches. Contemplation of death was exposing a very cruel interpretation of life, and she felt the ache that she was all too familiar with.

By opening her eyes and staring intently at the bedside light, Helen managed to wrench her mind away from this line of thought. But only for the briefest of moments. The light switch made her contemplate the probable existence of a 'life' switch. What was life that it could so easily be switched off? She could feel again the flutterings in her abdomen that had confirmed Martha's life in her womb. With Hannah, they had been astounding, but the second time around with Martha, they had been much anticipated and simply wonderful when they happened—proof that she was indeed a creator of life. Death had robbed her of this life and was utterly indifferent to her distress. Did life simply equate to an animating form of electricity that lit up dull lumps of flesh in the same way that electricity lit up the dull coils of wire in a light bulb? Was life just a mechanical process, a complex product of the laws of cause and effect? Was Martha's rich personality no more than an impression of individuality generated by a brain that was, in fact, just some kind of organic super-computer? And if this is the case, then what of free will, the exercise of which surely defines the individual? And if there is no free will, then there is no point of there being a purpose in life, because one is not free to choose either to pursue it or to ignore it. And if there is no purpose, the existence of God becomes a fanciful attempt to generate purpose where none exists. Phew! This was getting heavy…heavier than Helen had experienced before.

But then, perhaps, there was a comfort to be discerned in a God-less universe. If there is merely oblivion beyond death, then rightly speaking, how one lives one's life has no eternal significance. Once it is over, it is over. The absence of a cosmic headmaster judging every last detail of one's life liberates one from a religious guilt that confines one to the petty world of right and wrong. On the other hand, and as Helen had observed in her elder brother who had once drifted away from the faith they had been brought up in, the responsibility of exercising moral judgement without external guidance is not as liberating as it might appear when one leaves home for university. It had taken Gareth nigh on fifteen years, and two failed marriages, to recognise the freedom of wise boundaries. Amazingly, he was now the worship leader at his church.

And, with this thought, Helen found herself returning to her default understanding of death and life. But, was this her belief or that of her parents who had raised her? Was it true? Could there be an identifiable existence beyond the grave? Helen desperately wanted to believe it was so. But, she didn't want it to be what she had always regarded as the depressing reincarnation idea of the Eastern religions. Surely her daughter's soul wouldn't be incorporated into a different body? She wanted Martha to be Martha, and to look forward to a moment of re-encounter when, once again, she would take her daughter in her arms, smile into her eyes, and run her hands through her rich auburn hair. As her mind effortlessly conjured up this longed for experience, she found herself anticipating deep pain. Its grip would shortly be unbearable; it would wrack her being. So, where was it? What was it waiting for? She was taken aback. She could discern no pain at all, and instead, she found herself experiencing a warm certainty that was as sure as it was seemingly unwarranted. One day, in a place beyond time, she would hug Martha once again. How could she be sure? She hadn't a clue. Would she feel this way in the cold light of the morning? Who could tell? But right at this moment in time, she felt she had received an assurance from beyond, an assurance that she herself could never have generated. It was real. It was profound. It was even resisting her attempts to reason it away. She found herself drifting off in a genuinely peaceful a state of mind…wondering, hoping, and praying that the morning would not expose the cruel deceit of a dream.

As she drifted off, Nick sensed her breathing slow and heard the familiar sound of Helen asleep. He had not been asleep as Helen had imagined, but as he so regularly did nowadays, he lay there going over his life to date. He was going to be 46 in a month's time. By any reckoning he was half way through his life, and probably more than that. Furthermore, he had only twenty four years to go before his seventieth, and if he lived to ninety two, that would mean living for twenty two years over the age of seventy. He was thinking in these terms more and more, wondering where he was, and what he was doing. The other day, a patient had taken him for a whirl in his helicopter. It was the first time since the army cadets that Nick had been in one, and he had found himself mesmerised by the experience. Here was a vehicle that was just brilliantly flexible. It could travel anywhere pretty quickly, and very slowly. It could go up and down like a lift, as well as forwards, backwards, and sideways. It even had the ability to hang in the air. How smart it would be to be a helicopter pilot. Then it hit him. No way could he afford to pay for lessons, let alone own a helicopter, and—this was the painful realisation —he was too old to persuade someone to pay for his training. He, Nick Derbyshire, was a doctor. Whilst it was something he had pretty much always wanted to be, and was generally content with, he no longer had the option to switch. He was too old, and as he aged, so his options were tailing off. He knew medicine did not inevitably lead to practicing as a doctor. He had a friend from medical school who, on qualifying, had promptly hung up his stethoscope to pursue an alternative means of cheering people up. He'd become a stand-up comedian, and had regularly appeared on TV for a decade or so. Whilst Nick had enjoyed the fact that he had studied with a TV personality, his enjoyment of general practice had meant that he had never envied him. In the words of his uncle Len, he had been walking on the sunny side of the street—or had been up to Martha's death.

Now that the sun had disappeared behind the clouds, the cosy security of being a partner in a dynamically successful practice had become an uncomfortable goad. It challenged him with the notion that he was stuck in a sinecure of a job, and that he had lazily acquiesced in the fact that to be a doctor is to do good. The more he thought about it, the more he saw himself as an expensive sticking plaster—one that assured people that the state cared for them. He remembered a history teacher at school who had once challenged the class with the question of who contributed the most to the health of the nation. As an aspirant doctor, Nick had been infuriated by his glib assertion that it was the civil engineer, the one who provided an efficient network of drains and sewage plants, followed closely by the dustbin man. Anyway, he had spent fifteen years of his life listening to the problems of individuals who had the security of not just their GP, but of a massive health industry dedicated to the alleviation, and perhaps even the eradication, of their suffering. Immediately before settling down as a GP, Nick had taken the advice of a friend and had spent three years at a rural mission hospital in Rwanda. There, he had had to discharge patients from the hospital, not because they had been cured, but because their relatives refused to feed them. On occasions, this had proved fatal. The comfort of general practice in Hertfordshire had pretty much purged him of the trauma that those decisions had involved, but now it had returned to attack what his life had become. So much of it seemed to stem from his severely critical self-assessment of his effectiveness, not as a doctor, but rather as a husband and a father. Had he been a good husband? Had he used his *really valuable* philanthropic career as an excuse to dump the responsibilities of rearing the girls on Helen? One of these daughters was now dead, and the other was fast becoming a stranger—possibly because of another fatally flawed decision he had made. You're born, you live, you breed, you die. Was there any purpose beyond these?

Another university friend once declared that, as far as the universe was concerned, man was completely accidental. He had no intrinsic value beyond that of any other life form. At the end of the day, his sole purpose was to secure the passage of his genes into the next generation. The friend was a particularly enthusiastic fan of this last detail, and made no secret of the fact that he was doing his best to deposit his genes in as many females as possible. Whilst Nick had been undeniably drawn to this approach, he couldn't ultimately allow himself to treat women in such a manner. Becoming a prominent member of the executive of the Christian Union proved a successful way of managing the temptation. He had supposed that others, both friends and foes alike, would keep a judgemental eye on his conduct, and that this would help him to be good. After a fashion, it had worked, but in reality, all it had achieved was a postponement of what he was now going through. He was at last asking the deep questions of life and meaning, ones that mocked the glib answers laid out in the tracts he had once distributed in the student union bar. He was struggling.

One of the things Nick had realised early on in this crisis of identity was that no matter how tempting it felt, to get rid of God was no way out. Even if he decided that there was no God, he would still have to work out something to live for—some purpose that would enable him to make decisions. He would need a set of values to guide him in his treatment of other people, in how to earn his money and how to spend it. He wanted to know he was not wasting his life, that he was making a good job of it. But, if he was fumbling about for something as basic as a purpose, how could he even begin to assuage his doubts? If you don't know what you exist for, you will never know if you're getting it right.

This was his state of mind as Helen dozed off. He was growing more and more concerned that he was losing his way, and that the routine of general practice was ceasing to protect him from the consequences. Did the past couple of days represent hope? One thing Nick had realised over his years in practice was that human beings find their meaning in relationships. Irrespective of the physiological condition of a patient's body, her well-being is acutely dependent on the state of her relationships with others. She could be in pain and not suffer, and yet on the other hand, have no physical ailment whatsoever, but suffer terribly. Maybe it was the upturn in his relationship with Helen that held out some semblance of hope. It was also interesting to reflect on this in the light of Hannah's burgeoning relationship with the dolphins…

For Hannah, this relationship was just beginning to exercise her. The family had never had pets—Mum hadn't wanted them, and Dad hadn't been bothered. This was her first real encounter with animals. There were now two dolphins in her life, and she could no longer see them as animals. As the days passed, she began to believe that she was getting to know them. She imagined she knew what they were thinking, and that they understood her when she chatted to them. They had accepted her explanation of how she felt about herself and why; and furthermore, they fully understood why everyone blamed her for Martha's death. But they didn't. They were in fact beginning to persuade her that it might just be that others didn't blame her either. Perhaps her parents might not hold her responsible either, or at least no more to blame than they themselves—they were, after all, the ones who had let Martha go to the party. She began to feel a thaw in the relationship with her parents, and as she sought to describe her new friends to them, she began to realise just how isolated she had become. She knew, however, that tomorrow would be the last day with them, for she was flying home the day after.

This fact had prompted two fresh thoughts. The first one was the obvious product of any new friendship, namely how to deal with the separation. With normal friendships, modern technology offered a number of options that enabled them to continue to grow. Not so with the dolphins. It was as she recognised this problem that the second thought came to mind... what made humans different to any other animals?

At a fundamental level, she understood all life to be related through an evolutionary process, one that had generated an unimaginably rich profusion of life from a single source billions of years ago. She still found it hard to imagine her origins in the helium and hydrogen thrown out by the big bang, but that's what she had been taught and she accepted it. Therefore, when looking at the dolphins, she was looking at creatures who had taken the same length of time as humans to evolve. Whilst the differences were plain to see, the eyes of experience allowed these differences to seem far less apparent. So what was the difference beyond appearance, language, and habitat? And then, suddenly, it had dawned on her. The answer to this question lay in the very fact that she was swimming with the dolphins in the first place. This was possible because Nate and his friends had trapped their parents in the wild to provide entertainment for tourists, and then had managed to breed them. "Had managed to breed them." Here was a very one-sided relationship. The dolphins had been given names that they couldn't even say themselves. Hannah had refused to use the names after the first time because she didn't like them; they were human names for human beings. She had instead thought of them as 'two clicks' and 'squork', which was her attempt to use their language. But anyway, it was clear that it was the humans who were in control and not the dolphins—just as it was, she realised, wherever humans chose to live. And if you thought about it, humans lived everywhere. The dolphins had to be carefully looked after in conditions that were sufficiently similar to those of their natural surroundings in the oceans. Humans didn't need this. Instead of being adapted to their environment, humans adapted their environment to them. They could live in the Sahara or the Antarctic, as easily as they could fly like a bird or swim beneath the waves. If evolution is about being adapted for survival, then perhaps humans had reached the end of their evolutionary journey?

As her mind pursued this line of argument, she found herself recalling the account of earth's origins that she had learnt at Sunday School. This had been dismissed as fanciful tosh once she had learnt the *real* truth at *proper* school. But if you thought about it, wasn't man the final species to be created, creation's pinnacle? Wasn't he given the task of filling the earth and subduing it? Didn't this in fact tie in with what she was witnessing here in the dolphin pool? The only thing she didn't know, couldn't know, was what, if anything, the dolphins were thinking. But then, what was so special about that? Isn't it the same with people? There is no way of knowing for certain what anyone else is thinking or feeling. Sure, you could try to interpret their body language, but it was actually the same with the dolphins; their body language was as demonstrable as any human's. Why deny dolphins the feelings that we unthinkingly accord to people, simply because they are not people?

But as time with the dolphins wore on, a worrying thought started to nag at her. By the fourth day it was screaming. To what extent were their thoughts her thoughts? At first, the sense that they were communicating with her was really vivid—especially in the case of Two Clicks. There had been no doubt this was the case. Now, however, she was beginning to wonder. The idea of talking to animals was all very Dr Dolittle, the make-believe world of the six year old. Maybe her flakey mind was playing a particularly cruel trick on her. Whilst she experienced their body language, her interpretation of it was so subjective that surely it had to be the product of her own imagination. How could she be certain though? How could anyone ever know? Was she simply on a journey of self-help, and if so, she had to be lost because she knew she could never sort out her own problems. She felt an urge to get out of the pool. Was everything that had gone before no more real than the conversations she had with the cuddly rabbit that she was still attached to but no longer sought advice from?

That evening, she spoke at length to her parents about it all. They had eaten in the hotel dining room once more, and by now they had learnt that they didn't have to eat everything, even though leaving the food still disturbed them. As the main course plates were taken away, Nick had mentioned something about this waste, and something about humans abusing the planet. Hannah joined the conversation and started to explain her recent thoughts. Helen just listened in amazement as Hannah moved seamlessly from her deliberations on human prowess to her deep sense of guilt over Martha's death. After that, the flood gates opened—they had to be asked to leave the table by those who wanted to lay it up for the next morning's breakfast. They ended up in Hannah's room where the conversation continued for an hour or more before the three of them had an amazing cry-in. As he cried, Nick, the master of being able to think outside of his emotions, felt the smug sense of contentment that accompanies vindication. His belief that well-being was dependent on relationships was once again being proved correct.

"The purpose of life is to pursue happiness during our life. A good life is a happy and exciting life. The ultimate measure of life's success is the happiness in our life."

— Principle No.6, The Secular Humanist, Purpose-Of-Life blogspot —

Beauty

"It's in our biology to trust what we see with our eyes. This makes living in a carefully edited, overproduced and photoshopped world very dangerous."

— Brené Brown —

The smell was all wrong. It didn't belong to the waking up moment that she was used to. Even before she opened her eyes, Lydia knew that she wouldn't recognise the bedding, or carpet, or wardrobe…or anything else. This would be the first time, for sure, that she had slept in this particular bedroom. Her head was thick, her mouth dry, and her desire was absolutely not to take a look at her surroundings, but rather to disappear into herself. Though she could recall precious little of the previous evening, she knew that she had once again ended up in the bed of some man. There was an outside chance she might recognise him once she did open her eyes, but, in all likelihood, he would be a total stranger. She lay for several minutes, motionless, as she tried to piece together another disastrous night that had ended as had so many before. Somewhere close by, a radio alarm fired up and the pips sounded out the start of a fresh hour, before giving way to a mildly erotic female voice announcing that it was 9.0am, Saturday the 15th of January. Two things penetrated the mist of her mind. First, it was a massive relief to discover it was Saturday

—she didn't have to panic about work. This sense of relief was, however, rapidly replaced by a miserable sinking feeling. It was January 15th and therefore a depressingly pathetic fortnight into the New Year, and here she was having quite literally screwed up yet again.

Lydia's thoughts were interrupted by the sound of a door opening, and she realised that someone had entered the room. Again, she did not want to open her eyes. She didn't want to see the man she had ended up with, the man who had stripped her naked and eagerly accommodated her drunken desire for sex. They were usually triumphant for Lydia knew she was very attractive—her brief acquaintances would often crow about their conquest for weeks afterwards. She felt a presence close by and heard something being placed on a hard surface not far from her nose. It was followed by a rather flat voice asking whether she was asleep. Last night's man.

She wondered what he would be like. Opening her eyes, she found herself looking up at him. Instant impressions made him somewhat younger than she was, maybe around twenty five or so. Whether he was good looking or not was hard to gauge; the angle given her offered a view of not much more than a stubbly chin and a pair of nostrils. Instinctively, she checked to make sure that she hadn't popped out of the duvet, because, notwithstanding the activities of the previous night, Lydia was actually quite coy about her body. As she did so, she realised, much to her surprise, that she was still in her bra. In fact, she was also wearing her blouse…and yes, her knickers as well.

"How are you feeling?"

How was she feeling? Actually, She was more than a little

confused. Whilst waking up in a strange bed was depressing but nothing new, waking up wearing any clothes, let alone most of the previous night's ones, was a first.

After a pause, he indicated a glass of apple juice. He had made himself some coffee and had just been out to get a paper —she could stay in his bed till whenever.

Lydia didn't know what to say. How often had the first words she heard been something like "You were great!"—or some similar reference to the scarcely remembered carnal activities of a few hours before. The shame that she would generally feel at this point was best left hidden; a few enthusiastic platitudes generally sufficed to suggest complete satisfaction.

"Thanks!" she muttered, and then, rather than commit herself to anything further, she groaned half-theatrically and turned over, tugging the duvet up over her head. Last night's man moved off towards the door, closing it with a soft click. What did she think? She wasn't sure, but this morning was certainly different.

Her next conscious thought was that the clock she was looking at now showed 10:46. She eased herself up onto her elbows, reached for the glass and raised it to her lips. The sweetness of the apple juice was just what her mouth needed, and she drank deeply. As she did so, she began to take in the bedroom. Given her delicate state, she was straight away aware that the sun was largely failing to penetrate the claret coloured drop-down blind that filled a large window. It was a decent sized room and there was a good gap between the side of the bed and the wall. The bed itself was one of those that is too big to be called a single and yet would cramp a couple sleeping together—unless they were comfortable enough to spoon it. At its foot was a wardrobe and a chest of drawers. A chair, over which her skirt was draped, sat in the corner, and a bedside cabinet, which now supported her handbag, stood just to the left of where her head had been on the pillow. Beyond the cabinet was a door that had swung sufficiently ajar to reveal a bathroom. Lydia needed the loo.

She got out of bed and paused, allowing a head rush to disperse. As she entered the bathroom, she saw that it had no window and so she was faced with a choice. She could leave the door open and risk her modesty, or shut it and allow the small halogen spots that were sunk into the ceiling to assault her fragile senses. She opted to take the risk. After washing her hands, she squeezed a length of his toothpaste onto her finger and wiped it over her teeth. The minty freshness provided a welcome, though short-lived, respite from the appalling taste that the apple juice had failed to suppress. She washed her face, and felt better for it, but avoided looking into the mirror. She didn't want to be confronted with the face of one who had just broken the most solemn of all New Year resolutions before January was even half-way done. This had in fact been the longest she had managed. A couple of days earlier, she had, for the third time, resisted the temptation of a first drink. She had started to hope that she may just have cracked it. Who was she kidding?

She walked back into the bedroom, round the bed, and to the chair where she reclaimed her skirt. It was actually in a decent state—at least one good thing on a morning of uncertainty. As she contemplated her next challenge, the necessary encounter with last night's man, she got a folding hairbrush out of her handbag and attempted to restore relative order. At that point, she had to look in a mirror because she was about to say hello to a stranger and she needed to check that she was vaguely presentable even though experience told her she would be.

She was.

She poked her head round the door.

"Hi there!"

The man looked up and she entered the room with a beaming, friendly smile. Lydia was good at smiling and she had, over the years, learnt that she could trust its easy ability to conceal whatever she might be thinking or feeling.

The man had been sitting on a comfortable looking sofa with his back to her. As he rose to his feet, he turned round to face her, and Lydia found herself in the presence of a very ordinary looking man—he was, as she had first predicted, in his mid-twenties.

"What can I get you?" he said as he headed off to the kitchen area beyond a breakfast bar.

"More apple juice, or would you prefer a tea…or coffee?"

She opted for tea, and noticed that he wasn't looking at her as he talked over his shoulder. He was clearly not at ease.

"What sort? There's Earl Grey or builders brew, or I've got some of those fruit teas—I keep them for my mother when she comes."

Seeing his awkwardness made her feel more relaxed. She selected the Earl Grey.

"I'm Lydia. What's your name?"

"Kevin Butterfield. Nice to meet you!"

Well, what else could he say? Kevin felt desperately uneasy. Here he was in his flat with an impossibly beautiful woman who was some years his senior. The previous evening had been unreal, and he might not have believed what had happened had he not woken up on the camp bed he slept on when his mother came to visit. He had by now been awake for something over three hours, and to be frank, he had found himself increasingly irritated by the woman who had promised so much but had ruined his night. Not only that, but given that he ended up drinking very little, he would have been out running this morning. With her in his bed, he felt he couldn't leave the flat for as long as his Saturday five-miler took him. Instead, he had eaten a handful of cherries, made himself a tea, dressed in his previous night's clothes, and headed off to the corner shop where he purchased some milk and a paper. On returning, he had primed his old style espresso maker with water and a decent quantity of coffee and stuck it on the stove. Whilst waiting for it to produce its rich, dark brew, he put some bread in the toaster. After eating the toast at the breakfast bar, he poured the coffee into a mug, and headed for the sofa where Saturday's hefty edition of The Times lay neatly folded.

He had just been drifting into the Review section when he heard the radio alarm going off in the bedroom. Without thinking, he had filled a glass with apple juice—his favourite drink for the morning after—and taken it into the bedroom. The woman was, in theory, the phenomenally attractive one who had amazingly come over to sit next to him in a small cosy bar near his office, behind Charing Cross Station. It hadn't taken him long to realise that the unexpected affection was due to the fact that she was somewhat the worse for wear. He initially thought that this may augur well. It had, however, become increasingly obvious that she was very drunk. She completely lost her appeal when she vomited over the table, splashing him with her noxious fluids. In that moment, she had ceased to be a genuinely unbelievable prospect, and had instead become a dead weight, an unwelcome responsibility. He had ended up not just having to look after her, but at one particular point, to protect her as well. At 9 o'clock this morning, she was an unremarkable lump occupying his bed, a lump that appeared not to be enjoying the experience. He had retreated back to the living room and taken up the paper. By the time she poked her head round the door, he was attempting to read a serious book that, unlike the Times, was unable to stop him thinking about the woman in his bed.

He had decided that he would adopt a self-righteously superior attitude when she appeared, and on hearing the flush of the loo, he went over in his mind how he was going to react. When the moment arrived, however, she was back to being gorgeous—in spite of her raw, unkempt state. All his planned moves were mangled by her smile. She radiated an aura that is reserved for those few individuals favoured by the gods; those possessing the gift of true beauty. He had been dazzled, and now felt stupid, clumsy and wholly inadequate. "Nice to meet you" was all he could muster. A self-confessed nerd, Kevin was a graduate engineer working for Network Rail, and he actually quite liked trains—this woman was uncharted territory.

Shit! Pull yourself together man…act your age. She owes you one, so just take it easy. Put the kettle on, make the tea, and tease her about her head. Kevin—he hated Kev—often found that when he was nervous and wasn't sure what to say, he would gently rib the person he was talking to.

"How's the head," he teased. "Feel like lopping it off?"

Lydia replied in kind, indicating that whilst tempted, she hated the sight of blood.

He forced a polite chuckle and began to make the tea. He did so as noisily as possible, but Lydia rejected the hint and wandered into the kitchen area.

She wasn't sure where she was, who he was, or how she had ended up here, but now that she had her wits about her, she wanted to establish a pecking order…with her on top. She hmm'd, adopting a tone that established her right to pry and to judge.

A semi-condescending remark about the sweet nature of the kitchen area drew from Kevin an unthinking response indicating that only 11% belonged to him, the rest belonging to a bank—another sad attempt to lighten the tone.

Lydia headed over to a large sliding window that gave out onto a small balcony. The view completely took her aback; it offered a vast panorama of an area of London that she was disturbed to discover she didn't recognise.

"Where am I?"

Kevin had watched her walk to the window and been struck by the casually graceful way in which she moved. There was absolutely no doubting her pedigree. He could not in all honesty recall meeting anyone quite so perfect, and this was a woman who had slept in the clothes she was now wearing, and who was presumably still feeling the effects of the night before.

"That's Norwood Park," he said. "It's a great view from up here over towards Streatham, but I tell you what…it was a real bugger getting you up here last night."

Kevin had intended this as yet another humorous comment

and so its impact on her was completely unexpected. Lydia turned round and looked at this completely unremarkable stranger, and suddenly felt totally rubbish in every way imaginable. She was suffering physically, was distraught emotionally, and confused mentally. Her play of superiority had disintegrated.

There was a moment of silent communication between the two of them because somehow, Kevin felt what Lydia was experiencing. He wanted to say something but simply didn't have the words.

He was rescued by the click of the kettle switching itself off, and wheeled round to make the tea.

"Toast?" he suggested over his shoulder. "A dry slice perhaps?"

There was no reply, so he continued.

"I'm sorry I brought you back to my flat—I didn't know what to do with you. There was a bloke who tried to drag you off, but you were out of it and I didn't trust him. He said he was your boyfriend, and I almost believed him, but then his mate came along and joined in. They both eyed you up and down and it was all wrong. I stood my ground and they eventually pushed off, but I was then left holding on to you. I hadn't a clue who you were, but finally decided it was probably best to get a taxi and bring you back here."

Lydia's downcast gaze, her silence, said it all; a curdled mixture of shame and vulnerability.

"How thoughtful," she mumbled, with a hint of forced sarcasm.

"I didn't take your skirt off," spluttered Kevin after a pause. "You had gone to the loo and left it lying on the bathroom floor. I folded it onto the chair after helping you to bed."

Listening to Kevin's account of the night's ending brought

to her mind a vague recollection of sitting in a vehicle next to someone—presumably him.

"O God! I'm sorry…" and as the word 'sorry' tailed off, she realised just how sorry she was, but it had little to do with burdening this geeky young man. Instead, what she felt was the deepest possible regret that came with this morning's irrefutable evidence that she was incapable of becoming the person she so yearned to be. Lydia filled up and started to cry. For a while, her crying was barely perceptible, but then it simply exploded. Hearing the bizarre noise, Kevin turned round and found himself looking at what could only be described as an incongruous scene: here was a beautiful goddess of a woman looking about as pathetic and as isolated as is possible to imagine. He found it strangely shocking. Too embarrassed to look at her face, he concentrated on the hands that were jerking around in time with her convulsing shoulders.

Kevin stood there paralysed. Once again, he hadn't a clue what to do. Should he say something? Maybe he ought to go over and give her a hug? He would have done had she been his sister, but this woman was probably ten years his senior, and completely untouchable.

Lydia sniffed mightily, and Kevin suddenly had a mission to perform. With a sense of relief, he looked around, grabbed the kitchen roll and headed towards her, tearing off a piece as he did so. He held it out, but her eyes were unseeing.

"Here," he said, but she failed to respond.

Lydia was also unhearing.

He took hold of her by the arm, and at once felt the intimacy of it…weird because the previous night when he had had to half carry her from the taxi all the way up to his flat, he had felt nothing of the sort. Now it was different as he firmly guided her to the sofa and sat her down. Lowering her onto the sofa, he sat down beside her, and found that his arm had ended up around her shoulders. At that point, her trance-like state seemed to break; she accepted the tissue paper and blew her nose.

"Hey, it's ok," said Kevin as he squeezed her shoulder reassuringly.

Zero response. *This is feeling bloody awkward. What to say now?*

"Look, last night was last night and now is a new day!"

God, that sounded rubbish. Kevin couldn't believe what was happening. He was sitting on a sofa in his flat, with his arm round a woman of the kind found only on the pages of magazines, muttering inanities to her in a desperate attempt to staunch her tears. Although words escaped him, he felt compelled not to abandon this woman in her lonely state. He was trapped.

His mind was still working away, trying to make sense of the past twelve hours, when he felt her relax into his shoulder. It felt both awkward and good. He concluded that silence was the right response. He soon found his mind picturing the body that was resting against his, largely because he could now feel her breast pressing into his side. He started to wonder how things might move on... *Woah!* Sensing the initial stirrings, he was jerked back to reality. How could he be heading off down such a crude line of thought at the expense of this sad woman? He felt instant shame and mentally berated his offending member, deciding to think of Arsenal's fixture list instead. They were playing that afternoon...away at Everton. He tried to select the best team for the game and was soon lost in the exercise. Yes, he, Kevin Butterfield, had, aside from trains, two passions in life. One was forever destined to remain a magazine fantasy, notwithstanding the woman next to him, but the other was proving itself an effective distraction from the former.

Lydia's mind had been numb for some time. She had allowed her emotions to overwhelm her, and had lost herself in her sense of utter helplessness. She hated herself. She hated her looks —they had become a curse. She hated her job which she had decided was responsible for this curse, and she hated the fact that she was completely incapable of controlling herself. She had been here too many times to be able to harbour even the tiniest glimmer of hope that things could be otherwise. In all this, she had not been aware of the young man whose flat she had ended up in. As her mind began once again to take in her environment, she was surprised to find herself leaning, almost snuggling, into his shoulder. At least he wasn't trying to talk to her. She found herself feeling safe and secure in his company and so she made no effort to move.

They sat there, the two of them, for maybe ten minutes or more, both in their own way appreciating the proximity of the other. They might have sat there for longer had not Tom Jones announced that someone was ringing Kevin's mobile. 'It's Not Unusual' for a ring tone had seemed a good fun idea at the time, but now it was unspeakably embarrassing. Any desire not to interrupt the moment was rapidly replaced by a more insistent one to get rid of the Welshman. He reluctantly removed his arm from around Lydia's shoulder, stood up, and made for the breakfast bar where his mobile phone was. It was Simon, who had been with him in the bar the night before.

Simon Fielden had joined Network Rail with Kevin on the same graduate intake, and they had found themselves working alongside each other ever since. Last night, they hadn't been able to get away from work until well after 9pm, and they had popped into Gordon's for a couple of drinks before heading off home. Neither of them were party animals and certainly not after a 14 hour day.

Anyway, Simon had gone off for a slash, and when he got back, his seat was occupied by…a woman. A fabulous looking bird was, yes she was, she was actually not just talking to Kevin, but was draping herself all over him like a nasty rash. Correction: not a nasty rash, but a rather tasty one. He caught his friend's eye. Kevin's stern glance left him in no doubt that three would have been a definite crowd, so he had left to go home. He was tired, and, at any rate, he was pretty sure that Kevin wouldn't get anywhere with her. She was way out of his league—it was like Dagenham & Redbridge verses Chelsea. No contest.

Kevin ignored the call, and Simon left an obscene message that Kevin would listen to in due course.

He turned and looked at Lydia sitting on the sofa, and she looked back at him. This time, he was able to hold her gaze and it was she who averted her eyes.

"Look, I know this is none of my business, but I really can't see what your problem is." Kevin, happily, had never considered a career as a counsellor.

"Yes, you got drunk last night. And yes, I had to look after you, and yes, I was put out. But hey, that's ok. Admittedly, I was a bit miffed when I couldn't work out what to do with you, but once I had decided to bring you back to my flat, I just got on with it. And this morning? Not a problem."

There! That felt good to Kevin, but much to his amazement, Lydia failed to be cheered up and the sobbing started up again. *If a lady is upset, then compliment her.* He didn't know where he had read this, or who had said it to him, maybe he had just made it up, but it seemed like good advice.

"Don't be sad. You're still beautiful."

It was like he had just triggered a landmine that had been designed to blow up a tank.

"Beautiful?" she screamed. "Fuck beautiful!"

There was real venom in her voice. She was on her feet in an instant, moving towards him, her damp, puffy face now screwed up with deep, angular frown lines.

"I hate fucking beautiful. I hate fucking beautiful."

She began to pound his chest with her hands which, Kevin noticed in the midst of his shock, were beautifully formed and perfectly manicured.

Instinctively, he wrapped his arms about her, not so much out of affection, but because he was up against the breakfast bar —there was no retreat.

She struggled for a bit, and then went limp…completely limp. If he hadn't held on to her, she would have dropped to the floor. So…for the second time…he carried her to his bedroom, laid her down on his bed, and lifted the duvet over her. She actually looked quite peaceful, her breathing calm and regular. After a couple of minutes, he went back to the living room and walked over to the sliding window. He opened it, went out onto the small balcony, and looked out over the Streatham skyline. Not quite the rooftops of Florence, but he liked the view. It provided a backdrop against which he once again tried to make sense of precisely what was going on.

It was an unseasonably mild day for January, and the balcony was just beginning to come out of the shade. This meant that it was late morning. Since it felt warm enough Kevin carried a chair out, went back to the kitchen, made an instant coffee, and returned with the puzzle section of the paper. He enjoyed its challenge and was confident that its contents could occupy his mind. His coffee was long gone by the time he heard the window behind him being drawn back. He looked round to see once again that pretty face peering apologetically at him.

"Hi," it said. "Can I come and join you?"

"Sure."

Getting up, he motioned her to sit down and went inside to fetch another chair.

A minute later, they were comfortably seated, their chairs angled in towards a low table that sat between them. They both felt the warmth of the chalky winter sun, and in spite of everything, it was actually quite pleasant. Not only did Lydia feel that she now owed Kevin an apology on top of a whole bundle of thanks, but she also wanted to explain why she had reacted in the way she had.

When she had come to in the bedroom, she remembered the violent way she had reacted to Kevin telling her she was beautiful. She had lain there trying to work out exactly what had annoyed her so much. As she did so, certain stray thoughts that had become a part of her reflection on life began to come together. A sense of urgency overtook her. She desperately wanted to verbalise them before they disappeared.

"Do you think beauty is in the eye of the beholder?"

Kevin was getting used to the unexpected, but was nevertheless caught a little off guard by this one.

"I guess so…"

Well, that's what most people said, and people do seem to have different tastes.

"You said I was beautiful if you remember."

"How could I forget? It seemed you weren't too happy to hear it said though…"

"We'll come to that later, but when you said that I was beautiful, were you stating a fact, or an opinion?"

"I suppose I was stating an opinion, but, on the other hand, I'd like to meet the person who would call you ugly."

"So, in your opinion, everyone would describe me as being beautiful?"

"Yes. I can't imagine anyone describing you otherwise."

"So what you're saying, therefore, is that my beauty is not so much an opinion as a universally acknowledged fact, and that it is not subject to the eye of the beholder."

Kevin thought about this. He wasn't ready yet to give up the 'eye of the beholder' bit, but Lydia seemed to have made a point that demanded consideration.

"I'm not sure," he said. "Take my cousin, Keeley. She has a boyfriend who swears blind that she's beautiful, and I really do think he genuinely believes it, even though I think she's quite plain. Surely that's the 'eye of the beholder'?"

"OK. But if you were to compare her to, say, Jo Brand, who would be the more beautiful?"

"Yes, no doubt Keeley, but you know what, I'd rather go out with Jo Brand any day. She'd be way more fun than Keeley who is not only plain, but depressingly dull."

"Don't change the subject. We're not talking about attractiveness of personality, we're simply talking about skin deep beauty. You said I was beautiful. What makes you think that?"

"I don't know. I guess it's the proportions of your face—they all seem to be just so, and everything seems to be in exactly the right place."

"And…?"

"Well you're definitely more beautiful than Jo Brand, and I suspect that the whole world—even Keeley's boyfriend—would secretly agree that you were more beautiful than Keeley. But what about Gwyneth Paltrow? Aha! Now there's a point. Some would prefer Gwyneth, and some would prefer you. Now that is the eye of the beholder!"

Kevin felt quite good after that one. He was beginning to get into this.

"Ah…but," Lydia responded, "it's all well and good to talk about Gwyneth and me in the same breath, but you've forgotten the really important factor in all this. If you say that someone is more beautiful than someone else, and that in fact the whole world would agree that I am more physically beautiful than Jo Brand—you did say that didn't you?"

Kevin felt a trap being set but he couldn't work it out. "Yes. Yes I did say that."

"OK, so then, what is this thing called beauty that you claim you can measure a face against in order to establish whether it is more or less beautiful? And why, when it is meant to be a matter of personal taste, does the whole world seem to have the same standards?"

"I'm…not sure I quite follow."

"Do you ever get confused by the sizes of clothes?"

"Eh?"

"Do you ever get confused by the sizes marked on clothing labels?"

" Er…not as I recall."

"Well you can't do much shopping then, because it's well known in the fashion industry that some shops deliberately undersize their clothes; a size 12 is labelled as a size 10, and a 34" waist pair of trousers will be labelled 32". The shops do this in order to make you feel good. We're all vain, including you boys, and you feel better about yourselves in 32" trousers than you do in 34" ones. The retailer obliges, and as you try on the 32" pair and find it fits, rather than questioning the accuracy of the label, you get a buzz—your half-hearted attempt at a diet is actually working. The trousers have made you feel good, so you buy them. Unfortunately, not all retailers do this. So let's say you're trying on two pairs of trousers, both labelled 32", and whilst one fits you comfortably, you struggle to do the other pair up. Which is the 32" pair of trousers? How do you find out?"

Where on earth was she trying to get to with all this random junk about trouser waists? Kevin found himself as interested in Lydia's train of thought as he was in the question she was posing him. He wanted to find out more…

"Well I guess you get a tape measure and measure them."

"Absolutely! In order to judge the accuracy of one label against the other, you have to measure them. So, if you are to say that I am more beautiful than Jo Brand, you have to be measuring us against some standard. The question is, where does the standard for measuring beauty come from?"

Kevin was beginning to cotton on…

"OK, I hear what you're saying and it makes sense, but as you say, where do we get it from?"

"You get it from me!"

It was said with a surprising hint of disgust that added to the impact of a response that was plainly ridiculous.

"Are you telling me that you are the personification of beauty? Now I accept you are beautiful by anyone's standards, but to claim to be the standard by which all beauty is measured is perhaps a little over the top, wouldn't you say?"

Kevin raised the pitch of his voice as the question tailed off to make sure she got the irony.

"No, no, no." Lydia back-pedalled fast "No. What I was getting at is that I work in the advertising industry, and it is my industry that is setting the benchmark of beauty. We decide if it's cool to be blonde or brunette. We establish whether high cheek bones are in vogue, or perhaps it's full pouting lips you're after."

"I know, but you're only using people so I don't see how that changes things."

"Ah, if that were the case, then maybe, but nowadays we take people and then turn them into what we want. I'm not talking about makeup and hairdos, nor even clever photography. It's all about computers. Photographers are becoming less valuable to us when you can hire a young kid with a Macbook. He will listen to your descriptions and provide you with the image *you* want rather than the one the *photographer* gives you. So you see, we put out there, into the public domain, pictures of people that are not real—images that have bigger eyes, or longer legs, or higher cheek bones, or whatever. And often, they are even anatomically outrageous as well. And so the public judges beauty by our standards, and for the most part, everyone feels less beautiful."

"Ok, so I get the drift, but I can't work out why advertisers would want to do this. If you know it's going to make loads of people self-consciously unhappy about the way they look, it seems a pretty crap thing to do."

"Ah yes, but you forget one really important thing. How many pairs of trousers do you have?"

Kevin thought about it. He didn't have loads, but he did have…well actually, hanging clothes up in his wardrobe had become quite a squeeze of late.

"Quite a few."

"And when did you last buy a pair?"

"A couple of weeks ago…"

He could see where this was leading.

"So why did you buy them when you already have quite a few pairs?"

"Because they were a smart pair of jeans and they were 25% reduced in a sale, but yes, I know, 25% reduced is still a lot of money for something I actually don't need."

A quick question secured the information that they were Pepe Jeans, and so Lydia continued:

"So, if a Pepe ad showed you a pair of jeans and listed a price, you'd say 'I don't need those,' either because you have eight pairs of trousers already, two of which are jeans, or, if you did need some jeans, you'd note the price and head off to Asda and buy a pair at a fraction of the cost. So, what Pepe does, and it's really quite cunning, is they present you with a really attractive image. This image will involve a good looking man—Pepe have a penchant for handsome sportsmen. Given that they are involved with Red Bull Formula One, let's have an image of one of their drivers looking directly into your eyes. Behind him stands a drippingly beautiful woman wearing an unbuttoned blouse that reveals a snatch of her bra. She's gazing at him with that unmistakable 'I'm available' look in her eyes. The driver's wearing a denim jacket, and we are simply informed that Pepe Jeans are Red Bull's *Official Team Partner*. They've nearly busted the bank to be associated with Red Bull for precisely this image. It explains why the jeans are so expensive in the first place, but the bottom line is that it really does work. The message is 'don't you long to be like an F1 driver, because if you do, kindly note that they wear Pepe Jeans'. As a result, blokes will pay £80 or £90 for a pair of Pepes when you can get a pair from Asda for a tenner.

"What we do in advertising is make you feel jealous and unhappy. We have to create a need because you already have a pair of jeans. We've got to convince you that our jeans can satisfy a need that goes beyond covering up your legs. Only then do we stand a chance of persuading you to buy something you don't need. And how do we do it? We present you with a whole string of fabulously beautiful girls, and suggest that they are available to the kind of blokes who wear Pepe jeans. With us girls, it's all about making us feel ugly in comparison with the photo-shopped models, and then reminding us that we can feel like the models if we, like them, squeeze our butts into the same jeans that they wear."

Suddenly, something clicked in Kevin's head…and for Kevin, it was a great moment. It had come to him during this intellectual conversation, *and* at exactly the right moment, *and* it was a seriously intellectual thought.

"This sounds just like Plato!"

It was Lydia's turn to be taken aback.

Notwithstanding the fact that Kevin was an engineer, the face of his favourite teacher at school had entered his mind. Mr Trant taught English, but Kevin had gotten to know him through the school plays—Kevin, the techie, did the lights. Mr Trant was seriously mellow, not only because he was one of the few teachers to call him Kevin and not Kev, (*don't you just hate it when teachers try to get too familiar…just back off Miss!*) but also because he ran a lunchtime club that he called 'Agnostics Anonymous'. One particularly wet lunchtime, Kevin had decided to turn up, in spite of the widely circulated rumour that Agnostics Anonymous was a sneaky Bible Bash trap. He needn't have been concerned, because Mr Trant was, as ever, simply himself. The great thing about him was that he never tried to be anything he wasn't. That he was cool was the ironic product of not trying to be cool. Unfazed by any question that came his way, he was even prepared to admit it if he wasn't sure of something. This meant owning up to the fact that, sometimes, even he doubted the existence of God. The discussions were really interesting because they talked about the big questions, like 'what is the point of living?' Kevin was now calling to mind the occasion when Plato came up. Mr Trant had been asking how we know things. *What is good and what is bad? What is a fine table and what is a naff table? And…what is a beautiful woman, and what is an ugly woman?* Connection made.

Lydia was silent, her expression quizzical.

"What the advertisers are doing," continued Kevin, "is creating Forms."

Lydia, who had read History of Art at Warwick, was a little hazy on Plato—especially since she had never really studied the Classics. But she did vaguely remember something about shadows on the walls of a cave.

"Go on," she said.

"Well, Plato reckoned that, as you said it is with beauty, so it is with just about everything else. He said that for someone to judge the quality of one table against another, there had to be a perfect table. He called these perfect things Forms, of which there was one that equated to pretty much everything. He noted, however, that great tables wear out and eventually become junk, just as the most beautiful woman in the world dreads the day when her superstructure begins to sag, and there's little she can do to stop it. Plato argued that these perfect tables, and perfect beauties, have to remain perfect. They cannot be allowed to change, because otherwise you couldn't use them as measures. In other words, they can't be made of stuff because stuff is always changing. He claimed, therefore, that there was a parallel universe to ours where everything is made out of nothing—it's all ethereal or spiritual, or something like that. Anyway, because it's not made out of stuff, it won't ever decay; it is unchanging and so it can be perfect."

At this point, Lydia interjected…

"That's really interesting, because if you think about it, the ideal of beauty that we're producing is just the same. It's not real in as much as it doesn't represent reality. Britney Spears is photographed, but then the IT kid gets rid of her sagging bum and erases her cellulite, and lo and behold, the image of her is as unreal as the spiritual tables that you're talking about."

"Yeah, that's right," said Kevin who was suddenly beginning to feel quite intelligent.

"But how do we know about these *Forms*?"

"Aha, now that's the clever bit. We, that is you and me, are, according to Plato, spirits trapped in our material bodies. We actually belong in the parallel universe, but for the time being, we're stuck down here. Deep within our souls though, we have a subconscious knowledge of all these *Forms*. Whilst we don't see them with any kind of clarity, the fact that we are aware of them is the reason that we are able to make these judgements."

"Sounds just a little far-fetched to me."

"Don't write Plato off just yet. When I first heard this, my thoughts were the same, but then Mr Trant told us about the supreme Form. Plato said the most important Form, a bit like a god but not a god, was 'good' as in '*moral* good'. All humans can make moral judgements, and if we all agree that Pol Pot did bad things and Mother Theresa did good things, then we are talking about *Forms*. Anyway, Mr Trant used New Year resolutions to explain this one, and, as this session was in January and I had just failed yet again to do my homework on the night it was set, it made total sense. New Year's resolutions, he said, tell us a few things about ourselves. For a start, we all seem to want to be better than we actually are. And then, we find it really hard to be even half as good as we'd like to be. But beyond this, it reveals that all of us have a notion of what good is, even if it seems to contradict our natural instincts. Plato argued that because we are spirits, we naturally want to be perfect, because that's how it is in the universe to which we belong. Unfortunately, we are trapped in our material bodies in this material universe, and this is where all our problems come from. Pretty neat, eh?"

Mr Trant had gone on to draw a comparison between Plato and Christianity—this was about as 'Bible Bashy' as Agnostics Anonymous ever got. He had pointed out that those who took Plato's teaching seriously would be able to identify with some of the teaching of the first Christians, who also believed in a kind of parallel universe—heaven—where everything is perfect. They also acknowledged the vain struggle to be good enough, but unlike Plato, they had a solution which was complete forgiveness and divine help to improve. They also had a code for living that was both dangerously revolutionary, and eminently sensible, at one and the same time. Many of the first Christians had been followers of Plato's teaching, and had been attracted to Christianity precisely because it offered forgiveness as a way of addressing the guilt of messing up.

'That was a lucky coincidence,' had been the response of one girl to this. Mr Trant accepted that this was indeed a possible explanation, but that as a Christian, he had a different take on history. History, he suggested, is not simply a case of looking at who did what and when, trying to work out why they did it, and then investigating both its immediate and continuing impact on the world. He believed that there was a mega purpose being worked out, and that history, far from being shoved from pillar to post by random human acts and events of nature, was heading in a direction under the overall control of God—who had created both space and time. He held up Christianity as a first rate example of this since it had taken a shed load of coincidences to get from a crucified carpenter, and twelve ordinary blokes living in a troublesome corner of the Roman Empire, to today's worldwide church which has getting on for two billion members.

Lydia had followed this, and she had to admit that in the light of last night, it did chime with her experience—even if she didn't like the idea of parallel universes and spiritual tables. Nevertheless, Plato only offered an explanation, and she was not interested in the sad beliefs of a discredited church. So, with no hint of a solution, she remained stuck with her depressing self.

Kevin interrupted her thoughts.

"Do you fancy a pot of coffee?"

Bang on cue; she was thirsty. Was Kevin a mind reader, or was this an example of a coincidence? This line of thought could get a girl all tied up in knots!

"Ooh yes please…"

Kevin got up and headed into the flat, leaving Lydia to contemplate the world as it was that morning. She too had enjoyed the conversation and whilst he was absolutely not her kind of a man in that sense, there was a simplicity to him that attracted her empathy. She was warming to him, in a *platonic* way of course, and her use of the qualification made her chuckle.

Kevin brought the tray over with couple of mugs on it, together with a cafetière waiting to be plunged. As he sat down, Lydia decided that she needed to speak her thoughts in order to fix them in her mind. Now was the moment, not only as a result of the events of the past 24 hours, but more importantly, because this encounter with little Kevin was a complete one-off. The fact that she had found herself growing to like him was a shame, because she knew that after she had said what was in her mind, she would never want to see him again.

Lydia recalled her first day at her sixth form college. Her father was a Colour Sergeant in the army, and his regiment had been moved to Germany. She had just done her GCSE's, and, happily, there was a sixth form college near her Gran's with two boarding houses for the kids of families living overseas. She had been really excited about the change because she was interested in seeing what it would be like to make a completely fresh start in a place where no one knew her. She could decide what sort of a person she was going to be, and no-one would know if she was acting in or out of character. She was particularly interested to explore her identity as a woman.

Lydia had been a relatively late developer, and she hadn't started her periods until her fourteenth year. It was at this stage that her body began to sort out its shape, and initial concerns about the size of her breasts had begun to recede. Other than this uncertainty, she was generally relaxed about her body. She ate normally, and swam three times a week in the garrison pool with her mother. It was clear that her 5'6" frame was going to be well proportioned. Most significant, however, was the way in which her face was growing daily more beautiful as its features harmonised and settled down.

Some women possess a coquettish prettiness that instantly fills men's loins with the kind of desire that some might righteously try to resist, but that most gladly sink into. Lydia, on the other hand, was beautiful in a way that gently, softly, drew you into her aura. You would notice her face, and as you looked away, you would be compelled to revisit it. As you did so, you would begin to recognise a subtle beauty unfolding before your eyes, a beauty that somehow made lustful thoughts seem cheap and unworthy, whilst, ironically, making the possession of her infinitely desirable. She had in abundance that potent combination of grace and beauty.

When she had arrived at her new school, she was not yet fully aware of the impact that her appearance had on the male of the species. It had not really concerned her, and she had not had a boyfriend. Her feelings were now changing. Amongst other things, the magazines she had started to read contained loads of articles about sex. It was clear that this was one of the, if not *the*, ultimate experiences in life. At school, they had always taught that you shouldn't do it until you were completely sure that you were ready. She remembered being fascinated by an interview with Jerry Hall, in which she had described how, at the age of fifteen, she had decided that it was time to lose her virginity. Having selected a champion bull rider, she lured him to a barn. Lydia decided she would take advantage of the relative anonymity of her new school to see if she could get herself a boyfriend and discover where it led.

By the end of the first weekend, she had a boyfriend.

She had been somewhat overwhelmed by his larger than life persona, and not a little flattered because he played rugby for the college's First Fifteen. He was a significant figure.

It had not taken him long to move from kissing to something more intimate. Whilst at first she had enjoyed kissing him, she had felt a little uneasy at the crude way in which he had shoved his hand down the front of her blouse and squeezed her breast. Anyway, by the end of the first week, they were an item. Baz, for that was his name, was the envy of his mates, and Lydia felt really good that he seemed to be so pleased to be going out with her. She decided that Baz would be the one she would lose her virginity to, and so a couple of weeks later it happened.

There had been a party at the house of one of the day pupils, and a number of the boarders had been given permission to attend it. The drink flowed, and Lydia was pretty drunk. Baz had pulled her into the toilet on the first floor, fished a condom out of his wallet, and it had happened. She was struck by the trivial nature of the event, and her memory remained vague—save the mental image of a navy blue toilet brush that had somehow caught her attention during the act. It certainly wasn't all that it had been cracked up to be, but there was no going back. Lydia Bushell was now a woman.

Sex did get better, but it was always somewhat furtive in that getting caught would have resulted in expulsion. After a while, she began to sense that Baz was more interested in her body than he was in her. Looking back, Lydia was curious as to why she had thought that he was going to be the one she would marry. Their relationship had lasted for six months, and the last one was really torrid. It came to light that Baz was giving his mates the low down on their sexual activities. She had been really hurt. At first he denied it, but when she persisted, he claimed it was just harmless banter. In the end, she discovered he had started seeing another girl—they were apparently sleeping together.

"What a total shit!" interjected Kevin.

"I couldn't agree more," replied Lydia. "I spent a rubbish

Easter with my parents in Germany—and things didn't get any better when I got back to school. One of Baz's teammates, Luke, came on to me the first night back, and I wasn't sure what to do. I certainly didn't fancy him but he was pretty persistent."

"I know exactly the type."

" I just wasn't confident enough to say no and the alternative was to go along with it."

Two nights after hooking up, Lydia found herself in the gym store with Luke demanding to have sex with her. She said she wasn't ready for that, but he demanded it on the grounds that she had had sex with Baz, so what was the problem. Her objections were clear; she was not on the pill and Luke did not have a condom. One would have thought that would have been it. But no—he said that she could go and get a morning after pill from the med centre and with that, well, in principle, he raped her. Although she didn't resist him, she was very much having sex against her will.

This was when she first discovered her ability to compartmentalise her thoughts in a way that enabled her to avoid dealing with the pain of an event. It was as though she had a loft above the corridor of her mind, and this enabled her to shove painful episodes up through the hatch and lock them away. Although she knew deep down that she would find herself retrieving them from time to time, it was a solution that worked. It removed the pain of the moment without the pretence of having to think it had all been dealt with.

The next day, she had a weepy time with one of the school's nurses who was really sweet with her. She resolved to ditch Luke. He was really annoyed but she was furious, especially when she discovered that he had gone around bragging that he had 'shagged' Lydia Bushell. A couple of weeks later at another party, she found herself drunk again and having sex with Nick —another of the First XV. This time however, it had had serious repercussions for her.

That comment caught Kevin's attention.

"Woah," he exclaimed. "Things got worse?"

"Well," replied Lydia, "Nick had a long-term girlfriend, Dawn, who considered herself to be the best-looking girl in the college. She was mad with Nick for betraying her, but the little cow actually took it out on me."

"Crikey. What happened?"

"She made my life hell. She slagged me off in public, she told lies behind my back, and on a couple of occasions, she de-bagged me in front of others. It was really nasty."

"How did you cope?"

"I wasn't going to be outwitted, but not everything worked out. I thought if I slept with some of the lads, they'd be on my side. Sure, they'd come to me at the drop of a hat, but whilst they'd be nice when we were alone, in public, they would still laugh at Dawn's jibes."

Over time, Lydia worked out how to survive. She had few friends amongst the girls, and certainly none that she was prepared to confide in. The boys who chased her, in a sense, offered her not only a modicum of affirmation, but, ironically, a sense of power as well. Because the boys expected her to 'go all the way', Lydia occasionally said no. Nevertheless, there were times when self-loathing would threaten to overwhelm her, but the loft proved to be an effective storage facility—and it seemed to be pretty large. She also learned that immersing herself in academic work helped. It was easy for her to get lost in an English essay or a geography project, but most of all, she adored History of Art. She could bury herself in a picture for literally hours on end.

The University of Warwick was where she first began to realise that her beauty had become a real curse. In her first year, she had found herself in an accommodation block with a bunch of people who seemed perfectly nice, and many of them were good fun. Once again, Lydia had been able to start afresh and try to be the person she wanted to be rather than the one she had become. No-one had any knowledge of her past life and she found this liberating. Not only that, but she became very popular. People wanted to be with her and she never had to call on friends. In fact, it got a little tiring because she was finding it hard to establish space for just herself.

As for sex, she had decided to forego its dubious pleasures, and this turned out to be relatively easy since she discovered that she didn't miss it. She had plenty of suitors but she easily side-stepped their advances. She was used to the lads always making a play for her, which is probably why she began to notice Tom. Tom was a quiet first year student who lived along her corridor. He was reading Civil Engineering and it was pretty clear that they had little in common. On the other hand, he was a together sort of person in that he appeared content with himself. When his friends came round, they had fun without being loutish. Tom and Lydia would sometimes bump into each other in the small communal kitchen, and Lydia found their conversations relaxing and enjoyable. Crucially, she never felt he was making a play for her. One evening, they arrived in the kitchen at the same time, and since they were both intending to cook a pasta dish, they decided to pool their resources. The pasta in its sauce was ok, but if the litre of wine in its plastic bottle lacked character, it nevertheless had its impact on the rest of the evening. Tom was not a virgin but he was nowhere near as experienced as Lydia. Whilst he was overawed—this was, afterall, Lydia Bushell—Lydia enjoyed being in control again as she guided Tom through their intimate activity.

"You fell for him?" blurted Kevin, trying to conceal his envy —he was also an engineer, after all.

"Sort of; I decided to pair up with him and see how it went."

"And did it go?"

"Well, after the first year, we moved into a studio flat that his parents had bought as an investment. It was in a nearby suburb —very nice."

"Woah," thought Kevin to himself as he pondered what had almost happened the very night before. The thought of actually living with her was properly mind boggling.

"It didn't last," continued Lydia. "I met this American exchange student, Aldo. He was big and brash—very American —and he knew how to turn it on. Anyway, there was this departmental bash at the end of the Easter term. You know how it goes; I thought I had my boundaries in place but after we'd finished a few bottles, we giggled our way upstairs, and the rest, as they say, is history."

"What happened with Tom?" asked Kevin, somewhat reassured by the story's sudden plummet.

Lydia dropped her head.

"Sure, I felt guilty and lied—said I'd crashed at a friend's place. There was more to it of course. I suppose I actually looked for a way to blame poor Tom. I had only slept with Aldo because I was getting bored."

Tom had become a little too clingy and suspicious, not liking it when she went out with friends, and at times displaying a real jealousy. He was also massively sycophantic in that he would always agree with her and let her have her way. In a weird way, his craven compliance had left her feeling insecure.

Lydia spent that Easter break in Chicago with Aldo and moved in with him back at Warwick. Within three weeks, this arrangement ended. Aldo was an Italian-American who had the charm to woo, but a crass, chauvinistic attitude rapidly came to the fore. Kelly's floor had come to the rescue and during her final year, she had shared a house with Kelly and a few of the girls.

Lydia had tried to avoid Tom. She had moved her stuff out one Thursday when she knew he was in labs all day. When he had returned, he had been completely distraught to find her gone. The next day, he had waited for her outside her departmental block and had confronted her. She told him about Aldo, and when he silently froze in a state of shock, Lydia had turned and made her escape. Yes, she had felt terrible about it, but running was easier than witnessing his distress. He had been inconsolable for some time and one night, two of his friends had bumped into her in the student bar and had had a nasty go at her. Just after her finals, Lydia spotted him in the refectory and had decided to see if she could make peace. He was surprisingly receptive and they had chatted for well over an hour, during the course of which both of them cried.

Kevin was absorbed, half listening to the story and half

imagining what it would have been like had he been in Tom's place.

"What a pratt," he mumbled aloud, almost unwittingly. "His insecurity blew it."

"Well, I didn't exactly respond well either," replied Lydia. "Funny thing is, I never realised the truth of how men actually saw me. Tom never made a move because he thought I was out of his league."

"I get exactly where he was coming from," said Kevin with a slight grin.

"And because I wouldn't go out with any of them, I always had a few potential suiters pressing their case. Tom simply didn't rate his chances given the competition."

"But Tom wasn't all bad?"

"Oh sure, of course not. In fact I found myself quite drawn towards him—although he couldn't see it. I really enjoyed our chats in the kitchen in the early days. He obviously did too, but he never tried anything. I was simply too beautiful to be interested in him. He later confessed that he had fancied me from the beginning."

"He thought you'd never say yes," said Kevin quietly. "He didn't want to embarrass himself."

"Well, I get that now. Our first kiss surprised both of us."

That first kiss was something Tom would never forget, and the fact that they had had sex that night was mind blowing. Waking up next morning in her bed was completely unreal. At first, he had assumed it must have been the wine, and whilst she had been a little tipsy, amazingly, he discovered that she had wanted it to happen. Lydia had interrupted him at this stage to explain how she had grown to like him over time. What appealed to her was not his appearance, but rather his simple kindness, his integrity, and the sense that he was at ease with himself. Anyway, the next few weeks had been like a dream for Tom. He was now Lydia Bushell's boyfriend. At first, his mates were incredulous, but when they accepted that it was true, they shut up. He had enjoyed their jealousy.

Tom had wanted to know why she had decided to leave him for Aldo and was taken aback by her response. It wasn't that she had preferred Aldo, but rather that he had offered her a fun time at a point when life had become dull. Hadn't she liked the fact that he always did everything around the flat? Well yes, she had, but would have been happy to have helped. Hadn't she liked the fact that he always went along with whatever she wanted? Well kind of, but she hadn't liked the way he had become a push-over. Tom had remonstrated; he had been so scared of losing her that he wanted everything to be perfect. She had asked why he feared losing her? It was pretty obvious that she really liked him; for God's sake, hadn't she moved in with him? In truth, soon after they had moved in together, she had, for a second time, seriously entertained the idea of marriage. For a while, she had found the thought of being his wife and looking after their children more appealing than any notion of a career. Some vague instinct had told her not to share this detail with Tom, and so she had kept it to herself.

Tom had tragically failed to cope with her beauty—she was simply too perfect ever to be content with him. He had spent much of their time together waiting for the inevitable separation that surely had to come. In truth, after the shock of it all, he found he was almost relieved that it had at last happened.

As Tom rose to leave, she had risen as well and hugged him. The conversation had had a sort of a cathartic impact on both of them. It had cleared up confusions and thereby allowed them to move on from Warwick understanding each other, and themselves, a little better.

It had also been depressing; for Tom, in realising that he had unwittingly driven away the woman he adored, and for Lydia, in perceiving that men didn't see her as a woman with the same sort of thoughts and desires as normal women. She was some kind of freak. Yes, a freak. Her burden was her beauty which supposedly made her incapable of wanting to settle down with just one man. How could men be so stupid? And yet her move to London, and the world of advertising that was to become her life, reinforced everything that Tom had said. Lydia Bushell was, because of her beauty, nothing more than a challenge to be taken up, a conquest to be boasted of.

As the full enormity of this had dawned on her, so she had found herself developing a relationship with alcohol that she was equally uneasy about. Health issues aside, it started to lead her back into a promiscuous lifestyle which she hated. And of course, when drunk, controlling her lust was near impossible. She had not intended to talk about this with Kevin, but somehow it flowed. Notwithstanding the fact that she felt her looks were a curse, she nevertheless guarded them jealously, and blamed the alcohol for her promiscuity.

At Warwick, she had partied pretty much like everyone else but had known when to stop. Things had become much more serious in London. Over time, the drinking culture, especially in the world of advertising, was such that she missed the point at which she had become dependent. It was a shock when she realised that a first drink invariably meant that she would end up drunk. Occasionally, she tried to give up drinking for January, but up until this year, had never got beyond the first Friday evening when everyone went for a drink after work. She had become an alcoholic and was scared, but persuaded herself that because she could go several days without a drop, she was ok. She knew she wasn't and so she had started to try to do something about it. This was why her New Year resolution to stop drinking altogether had been so important. She had reasoned with herself that if she could stick to it, then she wasn't an alcoholic, and she could relax. But of course, linked to the issue of alcohol was also the matter of sex. And so here she was, sitting on the balcony of a flat belonging to a railway engineer who she didn't know, and to whom she had just exposed herself in the most intimate manner.

As it became clear that Lydia had finished, Kevin tried to think of something to say, failed, noticed that the cafetière had not been plunged, and set about preparing two mugs of coffee, lukewarm and black.

"I think I'll give it a miss," said Lydia, screwing up her face. "I'd better be getting off."

She indeed felt completely laid bare by what she had said —way more so than she had ever felt after sex with a stranger. Nonetheless, she was glad she had at last spoken her mind. In a sense, nothing had been even remotely resolved, but some stuff had been uncovered and much had been owned up to. Airing it all in a coherent way, to a stranger who she would never see again, had also been a selfish act. She doubted that Kevin would see it that way. Even so, she didn't want to make eye contact so she hurried back inside and fished her mobile out of her handbag. It was an *Uber* moment. She then went to the bathroom, had a pee, applied an acceptable minimum of makeup, and headed back to the living room. Kevin looked expectantly at her; he was sweet. He even reminded her of Tom, and she had briefly reflected on what might have been, but that was of another age long ago. She had moved on, and Kevin was not her sort. Nevertheless, out of politeness, she took his proffered card, mumbled a non-committal response to the suggestion of meeting up, and gave him a continental peck on the cheek. As she left, she flashed a brilliant smile entirely for his benefit.

Kevin stood at the door listening to her heels clacking the concrete floor as she walked away. He remained motionless until the dull ding of a bell announced the arrival of the lift. He eased the door closed, strolled back to the sofa, and randomly picked up the colour supplement. There, on the rear cover, stood the good looking, unshaven bloke, relaxing next to the *I want it now* beauty—oversized eyes, accentuated cleavage…impossibly long legs. He too smiled, not a flashy one, but rather one that betrayed the satisfaction of having seen through the deceit.

"It's in our biology to trust what we see with our eyes.
This makes living in a carefully edited, overproduced
and photoshopped world very dangerous."

— Brené Brown —

Descartes in a Car

"Cogito ergo sum"

— René Descartes —

It's strange, isn't it, how the most benign of habits, when interrupted, can rebel to the point where it lays bare the very roots of a person's identity.

It was a Wednesday morning in late September, and as he had done for the past three years, Martin Rossiter gulped the last inch of tea in the bottom of his mug, and kissed his wife, Elizabeth, on the left cheek. He smiled at Chandos, their five year old German Pointer, and walked through the hall towards the door.

"Goodbye Ruth, goodbye Daniel," he called up the stairs before leaving.

"Bye Dad, see you tonight," came the joint reply.

"Morning Neville, bang on time as usual."

Neville was waiting patiently at the top of the drive, right next to the passenger door of the Austin 10. Martin reached into his right hand jacket pocket and felt for his bunch of keys and unlocked the nearside door. As he did so, she who was about to interrupt his habit arrived next to him breathing slightly heavily, the result of mild exertion.

Ever since moving to Nosebury in the Autumn of 1940,

and prior to the arrival of this intruder, such had been the daily pattern of Martin's departure to work. Martin had met Neville in the Summer of 1940 at a Physics symposium in Oxford, and had been invited to be considered for a job working as a boffin for the government. Martin had jumped at the idea; he had dreaded receiving the army's call-up. As a happily married father of two, he had no desire whatsoever to risk his life on a battlefield. The recent crushing of the Allied armies in France had convinced him it was only a matter of time before the letter arrived, so he was delighted that an appointment to a hush-hush outfit ensued. That it meant the family had to up sticks from Lancashire and head South, to a small Buckinghamshire village near the market town of Winslow, was a small price to pay. The new three bedroomed house in Nosebury was adequate, and, since the government now paid the rent, he had been able to buy the *Goodwood* model of the Austin 10.

It turned out that Neville lived next door, and together, they would drive to Bicester each day, where they worked. This was as well because the Oxfordshire-Buckinghamshire border was completely unknown to Martin, and the absence of road signs meant that, had it not been for Neville, he would never have made it. From the very outset, Neville had proved to be an excellent guide—Martin merely had to listen to Neville's soft but authoritative voice, and follow the instructions. "Turn left here." "Straight across at the crossroads and then take the right fork," etc. When Neville was away for whatever reason, Martin was able to get to work but if truth be told, he never really understood his route in relation to its destination, he simply knew what option to take whenever he encountered a junction. If you'd shown him a map of the area, he would have been incapable of pointing out his place of work.

Life was good, work well paid and not dangerous, family happy and safe—the Luftwaffe had not tried to bomb Nosebury—and Elizabeth was content. Martin had met Elizabeth in Bude at the age of fifteen. He had once remarked that it was strange that, whilst both of their families had always passed their fortnight's summer holiday in houses not a mile from each other, their first encounter had taken four years to happen. Two years later they had experienced their first kiss, and the following year they had spent the entire fortnight together. From that moment on, they both knew they would be married. So it was that, four years later, they found themselves in Bude on their honeymoon—in July rather than August. They settled in Preston where Martin taught Physics in a secondary school, and as a keen walker, he regularly took groups of boys up to the Lake District during the holidays. It was in Preston that Ruth and Daniel, their children, were born. It had been a real wrench leaving, but the prospect of helping the war effort without having to risk his life had been too wonderful to turn down.

The work was intellectually challenging, and to his delight, Martin found that whilst there was variety, such variety was contained within a regular structure. It was in fact rather like being a teacher. Although work was confined by a timetable and lesson content, as prescribed by a syllabus, there was a degree of 'safe' freedom within these constraints. Ohm's law might not have changed for the past 125 years or so, but every class he taught it to was different. Martin enjoyed the task of getting to know his pupils, and took care to plan his lessons appropriately. Anyway, in the Autumn of 1943, had you asked him how his life was, he would have been unable to articulate more than the odd minor concern, for he was most content with his lot. He could therefore be excused for not anticipating the life changing impact of the woman who was now standing beside him as he unlocked the car door on that particular Wednesday morning.

Fiona Skelding was a lively, single woman who lived with two other women in digs three doors down. They had moved in during the spring of that year and Fiona had rapidly forged a warm relationship with Ruth and Daniel Rossiter who had come to adore her. She had often taken the youngsters for rambles during the long summer evenings. Like Martin and Neville, Fiona and her friends worked in Bicester, but they tended to leave later in a car driven by one of the housemates. All three of them worked for the military, but Martin didn't know in what capacity, nor was he likely to find out—such details were never shared with others. Even so, given that Bicester was not a large town, Martin thought it ever so slightly odd that they had yet to bump into each other.

Anyway, Fiona had knocked on the front door at 6.22pm on Monday evening, which was seven minutes after the Rossiters sat down for supper. Martin had been irritated to have to get up from the table. Fiona and her housemates had been planning to head to Birmingham for a day out on Wednesday, but something had cropped up at work for Fiona. As her friends were still going ahead with the plans, Fiona had come to beg a lift. After a quick mental review of possible objections, Martin could find none and so had agreed, and had informed her that he set off at 7.40am prompt. Fiona said she wouldn't be late. On Tuesday, Martin had been surprised by Neville's reaction when he had told him that Fiona would be joining them the following day. Although not overtly hostile, Neville was decidedly cool.

As Fiona waited for the door to be unlocked, it was clear that there was something wrong; Neville said nothing as they all got in. He was certainly not his charmingly effusive self. Martin inserted the ignition key, withdrew the choke knob and pressed the start button. The engine turned over for a few seconds before coming to life. After checking all the dials and gauges, he depressed the clutch, selected first gear, drove down the drive and headed for the first junction. Even as Neville intoned the instruction to turn left, Martin was indicating left.

"Don't you mean right?" came the female voice from behind.

"Eh?" said Martin. "No, it's left here."

"But surely Bicester is to the right," responded Fiona.

"Absolutely not!" interjected Neville. "We've been travelling to work together for the past couple of years, and we have always turned left."

"But turning left takes you off towards Winslow and Bletchley. You need to turn right if you want to go to Bicester." Fiona was sounding quite insistent.

"Don't talk such rubbish. What do you know? You've only lived here for a few months." Neville's voice was rising in volume.

"Well, I want to go to Bicester, and to get to Bicester, you have to turn right." Fiona now sounded exasperated.

"It's left for Bicester, it always has been and always will be!" shouted Neville.

"I promise you, Martin, I don't know where you think you've been going to, but if you've been turning left here, you've not been going to Bicester. If you insist on turning the wrong way, could you please let me out because ***I*** need to get to Bicester."

Martin had been taken aback by this somewhat heated altercation. Instinct told him that he ought to go left because he had always gone left, but why was this his instinct? If he thought about it, which he was now doing with a clarity that surprised him, Neville, the obvious source of this instinct, was, for the first time, not the charming individual he had come to know. This unknown Neville disturbed him, for it cast into doubt all he had ever thought about his colleague. Given the part he had played in his life over the last three years, this was worrying.

Which way should he turn?

Unable to come to a reasoned decision, Martin submitted to his initial instinct; he turned left and immediately pulled over. An exasperated Fiona got out and wished them an interesting onward journey to somewhere other than Bicester. By the time the door had slammed shut, Neville had already collected himself. In the relaxed, reassuring manner that was his calling card, he confirmed Martin in his decision and began to recall amusing incidents from previous journeys to Bicester.

"Do you remember the policeman lying next to his bicycle on the ground over there?" he asked as they pulled up at a T-junction. They reminisced about the bike's lorry-mangled rear wheel and the policeman's mud-splattered uniform—that and the fact that he couldn't stop laughing because he was dead drunk.

But even as Martin joined in with this cheerful banter, he just knew that Neville was trying to persuade him that his decision to drop Fiona off had been the correct one. Moreover, it was the very method being employed that was ringing the alarm bells in his mind. If Neville had simply rejected Fiona and her objections out of hand, then maybe the justification would have rung true. Neville's more subtle approach, however, was so entirely in keeping with the image he projected that Martin began to think the unthinkable; Fiona Skelding, in all her spontaneous innocence, perhaps bore the truth. Had Neville been deceiving him all this time?

Martin kept these thoughts to himself and participated in Neville's game all the way to Bicester. As was ever the case, that morning was a hectic one and he had little opportunity to dwell on the curious events of the journey to work. When he stood up from his chair to head off for lunch, he turned right when he exited the hut instead of left—which would have taken him to the NAAFI canteen. He set out into the grounds of the large stately home which housed the outfit he was working for. There, he found a small depression in a little dell, spread his overcoat on the ground, and sat down to ponder.

What had begun as a simple question of who was telling the truth—Neville or Fiona—was fast becoming a matter of fundamental importance. Martin felt himself beginning to be confronted by a crisis that went right to the heart of his very existence.

Martin had been raised by his mum and her parents. His father had found himself serving near St Quentin during Germany's final offensive of March 1918. He was a young captain in a battalion of the Manchester Regiment that had been cut off by the German Stormtroopers and had fought, almost literally, to the last man. Captain Isaac Rossiter had been awarded the Military Cross, posthumously, and Martin's mother had worn it on her dress every Saturday thereafter. Though this could not make up for a father-son relationship curtailed before it had a chance to establish itself, Isaac did, however, have an impact on his life.

Martin felt a duty to live up to his father's sacrifice, but whilst he was bright and hard working at school, he discovered, to his distress, that he was a coward. He first realised this when playing rugby at prep school when he found that he didn't like to tackle. In the ensuing years, he realised that in order to avoid conflict, the best thing was to go along with the dominant individuals in his life, whether they were the bullies in his dormitory or his mother or grandfather. The simplest way to achieve this was to avoid making his mind up lest he found himself at loggerheads with those who he increasingly allowed to order his life. Thus, Martin Rossiter became a master in acquiescence. As an approach to life, it worked so spectacularly well that over time he ceased to recognise that this was the way in which he operated. He thought of Elizabeth, his wife of the past seven years. They seemed to complement each other in as much as his desire to avoid the vulnerability of decision making nurtured her quiet assurance that she was always correct. When his encounter with Neville at the conference had led to this job, he had been so relieved. Terrified of being called up, he had been contemplating using his identity as a school teacher in order to secure an exemption. He'd tried to reason with himself that this would have been the wise course of action because the last thing a unit needs is a member whose cowardice would be a threat to the whole. Somehow though, he knew this was a cop-out that he would not have permitted himself. Neville's quiet authority in the matter of his recruitment had been more than he could have wished for, and the same authority had been good to be around on a daily basis.

So right here, right now, whilst Neville's authority was not in question, Neville's integrity very much was. The delightfully straightforward Fiona had challenged it, and this morning, Martin had to do something that he had assiduously avoided for so much of his life. He had to make a decision in the face of two conflicting truths. Not only that, but his choice had exposed the real motive underpinning his decision to fall in step with a dominant force—a force he now genuinely believed to have been concealing the truth from him. But what truth? The truth of which way to turn at a junction? The truth of where this stately home was? The truth of who he was working for? The truth of where he lived? The truth of who he lived with? What about the truth of his marriage? Did Elizabeth really love him? Were Daniel and Ruth his children? How could he know?

These thoughts were hugely unsettling because it felt that they were subject to no authority other than his own mind. Was this actually the case? How could he know if what he was thinking now was no more than the product of something his grandfather might have said to him whilst he was courting Elizabeth? For example, his grandfather had always thought Elizabeth to be a pretty thing who was used to getting her own way, and had warned him against the marriage. As that thought and others assailed him, he saw the full impact of the implications. How could he know anything at all with any degree of assurance?

All his opinions were clearly built upon years and years of input from others—others whose reliability in the matter of authenticity he was now seriously challenging. For instance, he was a great believer that in marriage a couple had to be completely frank with each other, so the fact that he tried to conceal his cowardice from Elizabeth made him feel guilty. But why should it? Who said that you had to be completely open with each other in marriage? Why did he think that?

So, Martin decided, there and then, that he was going to try and head back to the beginning of knowledge. He would start from scratch, and attempt to reconstruct his outlook on the basis of what he alone could accept as the truth. This is where I enter the picture.

Let me introduce myself. My name is Geoff Rossiter. Martin is my grandfather, or should I say he *was* my grandfather for he died last Wednesday, just three months after receiving his first birthday card from the Queen. I had always been very close to Granddad Martin and we had always hit it off. I think this was because he saw a lot of himself in me, and to be sure, I was fascinated to discover that like me, he tended to 'tin out of tackles' on the rugby pitch. Anyway, he poked me via Facebook half a year ago saying that he wanted to have a chat. We sorted out a date, and I arranged with the nursing home to take him out for 24 hours. By this stage, the growth on his left lung had been declared malignant. Martin had decided to seek palliative care rather than opt for invasive procedures that might have squeezed an extra year or so out of his hundred year old body. At this point though, he was still relatively fit.

Martin had wanted to go to Nosebury, and since it was quite

a drive from Preston, I had booked overnight accommodation in a Bicester hotel—the real Bicester that is. At his suggestion, we ate lunch in a pub in Winslow, a hostelry that Martin had frequented during the war. It remained largely unchanged on the outside, and still bore the same name—The Bell.

It seems that this had been the moment he had been waiting for; he launched into the account that I have just related. Up to this point in the story, it had been a simple case of him telling the tale, quite a bit of which I already knew.

"What do you mean by start again, Granddad?" (How could I call him anything else, in spite of being well into my fifth decade?)

"Well, you know how it is. So much of what we think is the case is no more than what we have been brought up to believe. When we question those beliefs, we often do so because of what someone else has said. However, how do we know if this challenge presents the truth of the matter, or not? I decided that I would systematically doubt anything and everything that I ever thought I knew until such time as I myself could accept it as being beyond doubt."

"Go on," I said.

"Well, that's what suddenly struck me so forcefully that day. Neville, who I had come to rely on as a source of truthful authority had suddenly had his 'truth' challenged. Fiona had challenged him and I realised that I had to decide which of them was actually offering me the truth. At that point, I recognised the far reaching implications of this train of thought. I found myself systematically doubting everything I ever thought I knew in case it was based on a false premise. It all kind of got out of hand. Maybe it was the intensity of the job I was performing, who knows? Whatever it was, it became an increasingly distressing experience. I was terrified of where it was leading me, and yet I felt compelled to proceed."

"But surely," I countered, "you could, for instance, trust the truth of the war that you were all tied up in?"

"But why? For me, the war seemed remote. It went on elsewhere, and was only conveyed through precisely the kind of second and third parties that I was discovering that I couldn't necessarily trust."

"But didn't you ever see bomb damage?"

"Yes, but how could I be absolutely sure it was bomb damage?"

"What about all those heavy bombers that flew over you on their way to Europe?"

"Not only did I have to accept another's word that that was what they were up to, but Geoff, have your eyes ever deceived you?"

This was an unexpected question.

"What do you mean?"

"One of the ways in which we engage with the world around us is through our senses, and I found myself questioning their reliability. I know that sounds mad. Believe me, I was in a very strange place that day, and in fact for some weeks after. I began systematically to dismiss the evidence of my senses. If, in the night, I could hear or see things that demonstrably weren't there, or if it felt as though my flesh was being tickled even though nothing was tickling me, then it was quite clear to me that my senses could be no absolute guarantee of truth regarding the physical world."

“Did those around you notice what was going on?”

“It was really only Elizabeth who noticed. At work, I was generally engaged in hypothesising, and so in a sense, truth was always a vague and elusive concept. With the children, their presence in the home was on the whole more insistent than my doubts. On the other hand, Elizabeth noticed my absent mind when it was occupied by neither work nor offspring. We had some big rows, not least because I found myself incapable of explaining to her what I was going through. A few years later, I read about an ancient Chinese sage who, on waking from a dream during which he had been a butterfly, had found himself uncertain as to whether he was a man who had dreamt he was a butterfly, or a butterfly who was currently dreaming he was a man. I was in that place. Knowledge of myself, I reasoned, came from two sources. First, humans around me reacted to me and acknowledged my existence, but I had learnt that none of them could be completely trusted. Secondly, the physical world reacted to my actions in a way that my senses detected, but if I couldn’t trust my senses, where did that leave me? You can see that I was becoming genuinely lost in every sense of that word. I doubt to this day that Elizabeth would have understood even the least of it. Suffice to say that, at the time, I was coming to doubt my very existence.”

“So what happened between the two of you? How did it resolve itself?”

“Well, in a sense, our relationship didn’t resolve itself. Rather, I changed quite profoundly. I had come to what I reckoned at the time was the definitive resolution to the question of my existence—it felt gloriously conclusive and massively permanent. It was on the back of that that our marriage grew stronger as the nature of our relationship changed."

By this stage, I was rapt. I was completely desperate to hear how Granddad had managed to climb out of the pit he had dug himself into. I forgot to say anything so I guess my body language said it all. After an agonisingly long pause that was probably no more than a few seconds, he continued unbidden…

"Well, it was magnificently simple, as so many things in life are. I realised that my doubt was the solution."

I was taken aback. What on earth could he mean?

"I realised," he continued, "that I couldn't doubt myself if I didn't exist to doubt myself in the first place. In order to doubt, I had to exist. I remember incredibly vividly the lunchtime that this realisation smacked me between the eyes. It was fabulous. Now that I was finally certain that I existed, I could begin the task of reconstructing my world by working things out for myself. In fact, I later realised I was, in my own way, following Rene Descartes, the Seventeenth Century mathematician, on his journey of self-discovery. His journey had emerged at a time when the Church's absolute authority had been destroyed by the Reformation. There were now two competing Churches offering conflicting truths, just like Neville and Fiona. *Cogito ergo sum—I think therefore I am* could have been my very words!"

I can honestly say that I felt a real thrill at this point. Yes, Descartes' saying was well known to me, not that I had ever grasped its meaning, but simply because I had often heard it said. Now for the first time, I understood its significance thanks to my Granddad, and it was so neat and so profound.

"But how did you go about this task of reconstruction?"

I asked.

"Well, you see, it was like this…I…well…ah…"

He was struggling to explain himself, when suddenly it was clear that an analogy had entered his mind.

"Actually, it was a bit like me and my first computer."

Granddad, at the age of 70, had been fully engaged with the emergence of personal computers. He not only loved them, but he understood them as well. With the benefit of hindsight, I realise how, given his work at Bletchley Park during the war, this should have come as no surprise. However, at the time, it was a source of amusement to the family.

"It was an Apricot PC running off Windows 3.1. The firm that had sold it to me had pre-installed on to its hard drive not only Microsoft's Windows, but also IBM's Lotus Ami Pro office software. From time to time, I added programs and then, when Windows 95 came out, I purchased the upgrade version and installed it. After that, I continued to install programs, and sometimes to uninstall them, until the computer began to crash. When it did so, I would have to reboot it. As this began to happen more often, I realised that in all likelihood, the installing and uninstalling I had done over the years probably lay at the heart of the problem. I decided to format the hard drive and start over. I saved all my work onto disks—it took me ages. I can still remember the odd feeling I had when I assured the computer that I did indeed want to erase everything permanently. It felt like a massive step into the unknown. But, having erased everything, I was then able to load MS dos. That done, I installed Windows 95, followed by Lotus Ami Pro, and then the other programs that I still knew I used. In the end, it was all reassuringly simple. Having started with a computer that had programs pre-installed on its hard drive, to which I had added and removed extra programs, I now had a computer that contained only those programs I had installed. Even though it was, to all intents and purposes, pretty much as it had been before, it was now one that I was entirely responsible for—rather than one that had begun life as a construct of others. Oh, and it now crashed not at all."

As his account drew to its conclusion, I realised what he was getting at, almost anticipating what he said next.

"So you see, it was like this. Having taken the decision to doubt everything I had ever thought I knew, and to subject everything to the scrutiny of my own mind, I realised that my mind had been conditioned over the years by the very sources of information that I was now calling into question. It was like relying solely on Churchill's account of the War to assess his contribution to its conduct. The end of this road was a systematic process of self-doubt that in turn led to the simple logic of Descartes' *Cogito ergo sum*. In a sense, therefore, I had formatted my brain and was free to reprogram it. Now, however, anything that went into it had to be passed by me and my readiness to accept things as being true or otherwise. I realised, for instance, that my senses were, by and large, reliable, not least because I seemed to know when they were playing tricks on me. People also, I realised, were thinking agents; they existed exactly as I did. So, whilst I didn't necessarily trust them as before, I did allow them to contribute to my understanding of life."

"And Grannie, how did that resolve itself?" I interrupted.

"As I became more confident in myself, so she began to

bump into boundaries that had hitherto not existed, if you get my drift."

"I'm not sure I follow you."

"Well, you know Grannie was always a pretty strong character."

That I did know.

"At first, I had been cowed by this, and had always ceded to her wishes. It seemed an easy thing to do, and I convinced myself it was the loving thing as well. What I realised was that far from being super confident, the opposite was true; she was looking for safe boundaries. That which came over to me as a desire to be controlling was in fact nothing of the sort. Rather, it was a continuing search for those limits that would define her security. At the time, I didn't realise the totality of this, but as I became more confident in what I thought, I found myself more prepared to disagree with her. Whilst at the start this caused some pretty heavy arguments, we soon discovered that these were constructive; through them, we developed the ability to disagree. And, ironically, out of that came a closer intimacy that…"

At this point, he tailed off and his eyes filled up. We sat there in silence and I reached across the table and covered his gnarled old hand with mine. Our eyes met—there was a knowing that makes me well up even as I write this. Anyway, he made his excuses and headed off to the toilet and I paid the bill.

We left The Bell and drove to Nosebury where we had a wander. The brick cottage where Daniel, my father, had been brought up during the war was still standing, though it had a conservatory tacked somewhat incongruously onto the back—an inelegant testimony to the fact that, for some reason, conservatories are exempt from planning restrictions. Granddad didn't want to talk, and I respected his silence as he took in the village that had supplied the backdrop to much of what he was now reliving in my company.

As soon as we got into the car, he started to speak once more, but I stopped him. I didn't want to be driving as he spoke for I needed to be able to concentrate on what he had to say. I looked out for a place to park and after a short distance, spotted a lay-by and pulled over.

"It doesn't end there, you know," he said.

"No, I didn't think it did," I replied. I had noted that, back at The Bell, he had hinted that his eureka moment in the company of Descartes had not in fact been the end of it all. I had been waiting for him to continue the story. Indeed, had he not piped up at this point, I would most certainly have interrogated him. Now that I think about it, Granddad Martin was effectively orchestrating this 24 hour road trip, and there was never a danger that he would have left me hanging there.

He looked across at me.

"You wouldn't believe the problems that accompanied my new, fresh, exhilarating approach to life. It all sounds so neat and compact, and indeed at the time, that is exactly how it felt. But, as the war reached its conclusion, I began to fear the consequences of a world in which everyone relied on their own intellect and reason to establish the truth."

"What do you mean?" I asked.

"Well, just like Descartes in the Seventeenth Century, on the surface, there was not much that marked the shift of focus in my life, save for the fact that I became more self-confident. By that, I mean that my basic outlook on life—that which informed the way I conducted myself—remained largely intact, just as Descartes had been a Christian both before and after his personal journey. But like me, Descartes had flipped things round. At the start of his journey, Descartes' 'given' was God. *In the beginning*, God as the Torah has it. He knew he existed because God had created him. By the end of the journey, however, his 'given' was no longer God but himself. Now, significantly, God's existence was something that had to be reasoned. In other words, had he decided that belief in the existence of God was unreasonable, he would have become an atheist, rather as many do today. Whether this happens or not, the final arbiter in all matters has become reason—a person's ability to work things out logically based on what is deemed to be *fact*. As a consequence, humans become isolated from each other, because what I conclude from being exposed to a given set of events might be different to someone else. At first, such a problem was a million miles from where I found myself in what was one of the most stimulating periods in my life. Not only had I discovered the wonders of self-confidence, but I had also helped to defeat Germany. I even came to see that my cowardice was irrelevant, and that it didn't matter that I hadn't risked my life as had millions of others. I was gloriously confident of the significance of the part I had played in beating Hitler."

"So what was it that made you question the long term implications of your discovery?"

"At first, it was confronting the reasonable arguments that the Germans had presented for eugenics—their programme of selective sterilisation of the disabled. This led to the killing of disabled babies at birth, and then to the selective euthanasia of the mentally disabled. The eventual culmination was the establishment of an industry dedicated to killing 'ethnically impaired' humans, as quickly and as efficiently as possible, in the attempt to refine the human gene pool. Hitler believed, I read recently, that future generations would thank the German people for having had the courage to undertake this unpleasant business of purging the human race of its dross. I found it particularly chilling that, initially, they never sought to conceal the truth from their people. Even when they were killing thousands a day, they never encountered resistance from those tasked with the jobs of planning and overseeing the process. I asked myself what I would have done."

"The ugly truth is that, on its own, human reason was capable of plumbing such unspeakable depths, and it terrified me as one who was in the process of committing everything to the test of my own reason. The more I thought about it, the more I researched it. I even discovered that Marie Stopes, an early promoter of birth control, was in fact driven by the desire to reduce the birth rate in slum dwellers. She observed that the birth rate amongst the educated echelons of society was dropping, and feared a detrimental population imbalance down the line. Like the Nazis, she pressed for the compulsory sterilisation of those deemed unfit for parenthood. The rationale was compelling—accelerate the process of human evolution by natural selection through the removal of defective genes from the human gene pool."

I had no idea about Marie Stopes, but whilst what Granddad said made sense, it left a big question. *What was the alternative?* I was curious to find out how my grandfather had dealt with this dilemma, and I didn't have to prompt him.

"I decided that in any culture where human reason is the only source of truth, a problem will inevitably arise due to the ultimate subjectivity of all human reason. Not only that, but I knew that even as I reached this conclusion, not everyone would agree with me. This only confirmed my increasing conviction that reason, on its own, could never form the basis of a genuine community. You see, I was using my reason to reflect on the impact of appealing to reason to sort out the problems of life, and reaching a conclusion that others—who were claiming to be employing reason in an identical fashion—would reject. This led to a further problem. I realised that all this reasoning actually involved a lot of soul searching on my part, and how could I be sure I was right and the others were wrong? I became terrified of getting it wrong and found myself drifting back to my old ways of avoiding decision making at all costs. I began to seek out the safe course of following the lead of others, because then if I was wrong, it was their fault and not mine. At the end of the day though, there was one issue that dominated all others."

I can say with absolute certainty that I was once again hanging on every single word that was issuing forth from my grandfather's mouth. I had no idea that he had been such a deep thinker. After the war, he had returned to teaching and had stuck at it till he retired. Teaching Physics had been his passion, and he found it hard to take when he had been obliged to retire at sixty. To occupy his days, he got more involved with the life of his local Jewish community and he set up a team to host school trips to the synagogue where children would learn about Jewish life and religious practices in the UK. It was hugely successful. Rarely did a week go by when one school or another, often making long journeys in the process, did not bring a cohort of youngsters to be entertained and educated by a jolly bunch of elderly Jews.

"And what was this one dominating issue, Granddad?" I asked.

"Purpose! Yes, just a single simple word, but of massive consequence when applied in a particular context. Our brother, Victor Frankl, had discovered its importance in the death camps. Those who survived were the ones who had a reason to live. He had observed that when a person lost his reason to live, he rapidly wasted away and died."

"The problem with having to work out the truth for yourself is that this entails you having to work out the purpose of your life. And the idea of a common purpose is reduced to a happy coincidence at best, but at worst, it is the product of coercion—whether by force or persuasion. I headed back to the Scriptures and to the Torah, and began reading once again that which I had been increasingly embarrassed by as I progressed through university. At the time, I judged it to fall well short of the exacting challenges presented by modern scientific discoveries. Upon revisiting it, I found myself sinking deep into its account of origins. I did this not as a scientist might, but rather as one reconnecting with the God who had somehow, in my mind, been separated from his Creation. As Jews, our identity is dependent on the belief that we are a chosen race, chosen by God himself. I believed he created the universe, but as a scientist, I completely ignored this belief. As I reread the accounts of creation, I connected with it in a completely fresh way and found myself marvelling at a piece of ancient wisdom. Not only is God proclaimed as the creator, but the purpose to creation is also explained. And, there is a role for me to play, not one that is dependent on me to work out, but one that begins with the words; '*Go forth and multiply. Fill the earth and subdue it.*'"

Granddad paused and drew breath. I waited for him to elaborate on what he had just said; I wanted him to explain how these few words from the Torah had addressed his problems. As the silence persisted, I realised that in fact, he had finished what he wanted to say. I would have to chew this one over, but I shouldn't have been surprised at this. Granddad would always be a teacher, and as a teacher, he knew that pupils best absorb those lessons that they have had to work out for themselves.

"We can go now."

He did eventually break the silence.

"Bicester here we come!" I intoned cheerfully.

"You'll need to turn right at the next junction then," instructed Martin Rossiter, with a wry inflection in his voice.

"Are you sure?" I queried.

"I'm sure."

And with that, he looked out of the window, and I indicated right.

"Cogito ergo sum"

— René Descartes —

Brothers

"Moral rules ought not to be such as to make instinctive happiness impossible."

— Bertrand Russell —

Be Warned!

What follows is a rather raw and at times explicit correspondence between two brothers in their early twenties. The letters cover a variety of issues, such as belief, instinct, and hope. These kind of merge into each other, and in and amongst, deal with the impact of casual sex on their lives.

I prayed, I agonised, I consulted…as I tried to decide whether to include it in this book.

Why is it here?

For a couple of years, I had this correspondence in my head. But, whilst the other stories flowed, this one refused even to get off the ground. I simply had no idea how to start it, let alone how to make it achieve the task I had set myself. Then one afternoon, I sat down and wrote "Yo Little Bro" and the bulk of what you have here simply flowed. At the end of the process, I had a first draft that shocked me. It did, however, feel authentic and it also reflected my frustration. This frustration lay with teenagers who, from time to time, would tell me that they didn't believe in anything. Often they were those who fancied themselves as individuals who thought at a deeper level than most of their peers. It used to really bug me. I would point out to them a whole host of things that they did believe in, and that if they didn't unthinkingly exercise faith on a regular basis, life would become incredibly awkward. I used to teach a lesson on Nihilism to the Upper Sixth, and the implications of not believing in anything, by introducing them to the brothers whose stories I have here turned into a correspondence. So, perhaps the fact that this story is somewhat *in your face* is a reflection of my irritation at being told "I don't believe in anything Rev J!"

So read it if you will, but please feel no obligation to do so.

Yo Little Bro!

How are you? How's Oxford? So chuffed that you finally got there and to do PPE[1] as well! How does it feel to be at the finest university in the world? What's college like? It must be grand to live in one of the old ones on the High. What was freshers' week like? Hectic I would imagine...it was for me. Though, to be honest, I can't remember long stretches of it. What are the chicks like? I tell you mate, the nerdier they are, the hotter they are. Go for the ones in glasses. You know you're in if they take them off to look at you, rather than stare at you over the top of the rims. Get going bro, and I want a blow by blow account of everything!

I don't know if Mum or Dad (if he was sober enough to speak) have told you that I'm off to Kuwait City next week. It seems like it's full of booby traps that Saddam's people left behind when they left in a hurry. A security firm contacted my bomb disposal regiment, and a few of us put our names forward. The firm's taking three of us and you won't believe it—I'm getting $250,000 for a six month contract... tax free! Do you remember Dave, my TA[2] friend? He's a BDO[3] like me, and he went out with the regulars last year at the start of Desert Storm[4] and earned his army pay. I'm off as

---

1. Philosophy, Politics, and Economics—a popular subject combination at Oxford and the choice of many aspirant politicians and journalists.
2. Territorial Army. The reserve army in the UK.
3. Bomb Disposal Officer…someone who qualifies to make bombs safe.
4. The codename for the first Gulf War, 1990-1.

a civvie contractor and will get in six months five times what he earned during his nine months—and no-one will be shooting at me! Not only that, but they're putting us up in a posh hotel, all expenses paid. Work wouldn't let me have six months off, so I told them to sod off. I've handed in my notice and I'm on the plane. The good thing is that the two other BDO's from the regiment who are coming with me are good people. Trevor is really experienced; he's an ex-regular WO2[5] who did loads of tours in Northern Ireland. Kirstie on the other hand is actually a solicitor in real life, but she's persuaded her firm to give her six months unpaid leave. She was on my course at Chattenden. One of the instructors said she had been the best reservist he had ever trained, and she's not bad looking either. (So do I fancy my chances? Why not!!!)

Anyway, getting my shit together and flying out—first class—next Monday. I'm not sure what my address will be once I'm out there, but I'll let Mum know and she can pass it on to you. Please do keep in touch.

As ever,
Nick.

5. Warrant Officer 2nd Class.

Hi Nick,

Hey, that sounds amazing—and exciting. You'll be out there by now—sorry about the delay. Freshers' week was ok, but not what you built it up to be, and I have to say that I do actually remember all of it! Just had my first tutorial and feeling a little overwhelmed. The tutor was chatty until we got down to business. He gave me an essay title to write down, offered a handout with a great long reading list for this particular paper, and suggested a few other books too. He then said, "see you next week." That was it. I've found one of the books in the college library and reserved another, but it won't come in till the day before my next tute. The librarian was really helpful though, and showed me the index of journals. She suggested the ones that would be most likely to help for my particular topic—it's on Aquinas and Aristotle. I have a lot of reading to do!

What is total rubbish, though, is my accommodation. I'm not in college—I can't believe it! College has this butt ugly block at the bottom of the Cowley Rd. It's white concrete and glass—anonymous, modern, and all right-angles. I so wanted to be in a room up a staircase, off one of the quads. I'm really pissed off. Some of the people are ok, but the others doing PPE are Rory, Charlotte and Jules. They're public school wankers and, for the most part, completely absorbed in themselves. They seem to view me as a nasty piece of shit that's had the temerity to invade their rarefied domain, and you know what, sometimes I feel like it. Oh, and they're the ones with the rooms off the quads.

There are some good guys here though, and as you say, some pretty hot chicks. But, I'm not sure I can be bothered. Working this Summer as a rep in Majorca, the girls were on tap. I could have as much as I wanted, pretty much whenever I wanted. I went there for sex, and for sure, if you want sex, being a rep has just got to be it. You get first options on the girls because you're sober most of the time, and they're too pissed to care. At any rate, most of them want it big time. All of us reps were up for it as well, and at first, I reckon I fucked most days—some days more than once. To be sure, I tried out pretty much everything you could imagine…and I mean everything. Well why not? I even had a go with another bloke. We were going two up on this chick, and when she passed out, we just carried on with each other. We were pretty pissed though. Anyway, by the end of the season I had gotten bored with sex. If you'd asked me what I wanted when I arrived in Majorca in April, then I'd have said precisely what I ended up getting. After a couple of months, it just got boring, so I started to target specific individuals. I found myself going for the ones who looked the most nervous—the hard to get ones. The challenge became everything. I was pretty good until it all fell apart with one particular girl. Becky was from Cardiff, and having done her A levels, was on holiday with five girlfriends. She was not particularly pretty, and had a fair few zits, but she felt innocent, and it was as though she was on the wrong holiday. As her friends knocked back the pina coladas, she sipped hers, and when they went off with lads, she would head off back to her room. Woah! This was a challenge, and I was up for it.

I quickly realised that I had to be cool and friendly and to appear not to want it. You know what, I nailed it— and her. I gradually gained her confidence by not pressing her. I was her friend. Genius! And then on her penultimate night, I decided the time had come. I managed to get her pissed, and, urged on by her friends, I took her to my room. But, in my moment of triumph, I suddenly realised what I was doing. She winced as I entered her, and I saw a disjointed uncertainty in her eyes. I had no interest in this girl other than wanting to shag her, and I'd picked her out precisely because she didn't want to.

Looking back, I think she could well have decided that maybe this was it. That perhaps she had found her man and that love was in the air. I had pretended to offer her friendship. Can there be a greater betrayal? How had I become such a sour bastard? She was not so drunk as to not know what had happened. I can still picture her pathetically trying to cover up her naked body after I rolled off her. As she did so, I saw a trickle of blood seeping down between her thighs. Another person's life was being fucked up simply so I could prove to myself that I could pull anyone. For the first time, I didn't know what to do. I just lay there, avoiding eye contact as she put her clothes back on and left. The next day, I threw a sickie because I didn't want to see her ever again. She actually asked for me and then, a week later, I got a letter from her asking if I wanted to meet up. The poor girl still thought I wanted to be her friend! I've never felt so shit in all my life.

You know, all this sex stuff, it's just hype. It is so not what everyone claims it is. It's nothing but using and being used, and it's not even all that exciting if one steps back from all the loose talk and thinks about it. Worst of all though, we end up treating our conquests as lumps of meat. Gavin, one of the resort managers—who's married—was one of the worst. He called it a "posh wank". It was not making love, which he said he had only done with his wife —who was at home with their two sons. I did once ask him if his wife knew about his theory. He told me where to get off. So maybe that's why freshers' week was nothing special —I simply don't have the desire any longer.

But so what, I've some books to read and an essay to write, so I'd better crack on. May all the explosives prove to be inert and the bombs turn out duds.

Cheers,
Pete.

Yo, Little Bro!

Thanks for the letter. It was great to get it because there's not a fat lot to do out here during our rest periods except read day old papers. How much better to read a letter, but strewth, it blew me away what you wrote about Majorca. Do I get what you wrote? Yes I think I do, but what surprised me is that you're a great guy, by far the kindest in our family. I would never have thought you could have acted in that way in the first place. I tell you though, if that was an eye-opener for you, my eyes are being assaulted by this place. Saddam is a total shit, and his soldiers are too. You know what, I can't even think of a word that adequately describes the men who have done the things we're bumping into here in Kuwait City. Kirstie has had real problems, and at the moment is working out whether she can stick it out. We desperately need her skills though. Trevor, our team leader, is trying to work out how he can keep her away from the horrors.

Let me take you to where I am. Saddam's soldiers have basically been able to do whatever they've wanted—and they have. In fact, what you discovered about yourself in Majorca is sort of like what Saddam's men are like, but so much worse. It's almost too much to believe at times. Imagine you're in a foreign city, you have a gun, and you can do as you like. Also, you come from a culture that seems to treat its women like shit. Now you begin to get a faint whiff of what we're up to our necks in. Basically, we're clearing buildings one by one and regularly coming across dead bodies, both women and men—even girls and boys. They've been abused in every way you can imagine, and in some ways so grotesque that if you hadn't seen it, you could never have believed it. You know those movies where people vomit when they see something? I always thought that was bullshit until I found myself vomiting before I knew what I was doing. Trevor held it back...just. Kirstie properly flipped and that's been her for a while.

So it's like this: the whole city is booby-trapped and you have to be so careful at every step. Trevor is amazing; he has a sixth sense, as does Kirstie—that's why we don't want to lose her. But, you have a door and when you finally open it, you're confronted by a naked corpse. It's bound by barbed wire and dangling upside down—like a dummy out of Friday the 13th except this is for real. What kind of a human being can do this sort of thing? Loads of Saddam's men, are, one assumes, husbands and fathers. How can they? And the bastards are trying to kill us all the time with their little devices. Fortunately, so far so good—most have been quite crude. But, what happens if we come across a sophisticated one? I guess if we do, there's a chance we'll never know it! $250,000 is bargain basement for what we're doing. SHIT. Don't tell the parents—they don't need to know. I'm just so grateful to be working alongside Trev. He's quite literally a life saver.

Enough! What of you my bro? How's it going? Public school wankers, eh? You'll just have to let them get on with their games, though take it from me, that kind make really useful friends. They have loads of contacts through their old boys network. Think about it. It might be a real help to you down the line if you have one or two of them on side.

Anyways, take care of yourself Pete.

As ever,

Nick.

Hi Nick,

This place is really pissing me off! My tutor's a complete pratt. His head is so far up his arse that it's a surprise that he can even see me when I enter his study. I did a shed load of reading on Aristotle and Aquinas, and wrote what I thought was a half decent essay. I enter his study feeling pretty good. "Sit down and read it to me then," he says as he looks up from his desk—before he's even had the grace to say hello. He's clearly busy with something else, because as I start to read, he's back at his desk. There's something on his computer screen that he finds more interesting than my essay. After a minute or so, he leaves his desk and moves to the sofa opposite the one I'm on, and peers at me over the top of his specs. I carry on reading. It takes me, I guess, around 20 minutes or so, and as I finish, I look up at him expectantly. He's looking at a journal on the sofa next to him. He switches his attention to me, smiles, and asks me what I think of my first effort. I'm not expecting this, and I mumble something along the lines that I think I've done okay. He tuts theatrically and lays into me. One of the sources I used is clearly one he dislikes. So, without reference to anything else, and ignoring whole swathes of what I've written, he rips the essay to pieces. I start to protest, and he shuts me up with a wave of his hand. "Look," I say, "read the essay for yourself". "No thanks," he replies. "I have no desire to read ill-informed diarrhoea. Rewrite it using that book," he says, throwing a gesture toward a messy pile on his desk, and without so much as a pause for breath, he continues; "Your next essay is on…" He gives me another title and a verbally delivered 'supplementary' reading list, most of which I fail to write down. And just as I'm about to ask him to repeat himself, he's said goodbye and is back staring at the green screen on his desk. I walk out in a state of shock — this I was not expecting. As I leave the college, I pass a mate who's also first year, but who's got a room in one of the college quads. 'Why him?' I ask myself as I pass the porter's lodge. Turning left down the High Street, I head for my concrete box.

I rewrote the essay using the source he referred me to. Although you get a week to do it in, it was no easy task to do that, as well as to read for and write the second essay. The librarian, Janice, really is fab. She was most sympathetic about my tutor who has a reputation for grinding his first year tutees. Apparently, it's good for us. It doesn't matter how good your first essay is, he'll always get you to rewrite it. She also helped with the reading list for my second essay, but because I have my tutes on Fridays, most of the books I want have been borrowed by Rory, Charlotte and Jules. Anyway, the second essay does not have to be repeated, but I almost flip when he shows no interest in my rewrite. There's no time for me to read both it and the second essay. And no, he doesn't want me to hand it in for he has no time in his packed weekly schedule to read it. He trusts that I have made a fair effort. What a total shit.

And you know what, as a result of all this, I'm finding

that I want to have less and less to do with this shitty college. In a sense, I know this is totally irrational, because others seem to be having a great time. I'm not, and I'm getting a real sad-on.

As I write this, I suddenly realise that I haven't responded to what you last wrote about, i.e. the crap that is filling your life at the moment. It sounds really grim, and as you suggest, I find it hard to take in what you've written. I guess I've seen that kind of shit in the cinema, but you telling me that not only does it happen in life, but that you are in the thick of, it is a real shocker. Don't know what to say, except that I hope you're OK as I write this. You're bound to have seen the worst of it, and I trust you're enjoying working out how you're going to spend your cash when you get home. Looking forward to helping you, bro!!

Better get back to my essay…Locke and Hume this time.

Cheers,
Pete

Pete,

I've just read the enclosed letter through, and it is grossly unfair of me to even contemplate sending it to you, let alone actually to do so. Please feel free to throw it in the bin, or better still, burn it so you won't be able to read it. I really don't mind if you do, in fact, I'll make it my request to you. Whilst it has been therapeutic for me to write this down, place in an envelope, and post it to you, you reading it will not serve any purpose.

PLEASE DESTROY THIS LETTER WITHOUT READING ANY FURTHER.

Do as I ask, Pete.

Cheers,

Nick

Kirstie's been blown up.

This bastard of a Kuwaiti soldier has slapped a 'Cleared' sign on a door. Kirstie opens it and bang. Right now, he's in a half-dead coma put there by Trevor who turned into an animal. We had to drag him off, though we waited for a minute or two before we did so. But Kirstie has lost most of a hand and both legs, one below and one above the knee. Shit, I had gotten off with her the night before and she had been so hot. I think we were both desperate for it because we had had a real crappy day.

The problem with booby traps is that they use your instinct to kill you. Put simply, it's dark, you see a light switch and instinct says it will make you safer because you'll be able to see. NO! It'll fucking kill you. It's not a light switch, it's a fucking trigger. Yesterday, a couple of cloggies[6] we work with were blown up. One of them was inspecting a door, and when he tried the handle, he heard a tell-tale click followed by a fizz. He yelled "Bomb!" and they both dived into a near-by ditch. The bomb wasn't behind the door, it was in the ditch.

Anyway, Kirstie and I were trying to wind down that evening. We were having a few beers, trying to work through what had happened to the cloggies and what it meant for us. Then she looks at me and I knew that we were going to. In spite of the fact that she has a boyfriend in London and they write all the time, there was a need to cling to someone. Both of us needed to, and so we did. "You never know what might happen to us tomorrow, we might

---

6. Cloggies…Dutch Marines.

get blown up." She actually said it as we started to get it on.

I'm losing it, bro. I'm not sure I can do this for much longer. Kirstie's not dead, she's going to live, but what sort of a life is she going to have? Will her boyfriend stick by a legless torso? Will he know that her final able-bodied act the night before was fucking my balls off. I'm scared that I'm going to make a mistake, and in a sense, I don't mind so much if it blows me up — my error, my life. But Trev has a wife and kids, and Kirstie's already fucked.

Sorry to dump all this shit on you...but I need to off-load, and you're the only one I feel safe doing it to. Writing it down helps...I think.

Nick,

I kind of did as you asked: I started to read the rest of the letter but then felt guilty. After the first few sentences though, I stopped myself and read no further. But, just as I was about to set fire to it, "fucking my balls off" caught my attention, and I couldn't help myself. But, at least no-one else will get to read it; I've now rinsed the ashes down the sink.

At first, I was glad I read it, but I'm not so sure now. What you wrote has collided with a whole train of thought that's been wearing me down of late. Up to now, I've not been sure where the train has been taking me to, but now I think I do know and I'm not sure I like it.

Whenever I think about Majorca, I get upset about what I did. What gets me is that for the most part, I was actually a damn good rep. I would put myself out for the guests, and I was genuinely warm. Some of the other reps were often reluctant to fulfil even the basic obligations of the role, whereas I was always happy to go the extra mile and I frequently did so. The feedback forms really rated me, so how come I could be a five-star warm friendly host and at the same time a predatory arsehole? How could such different personalities exist side-by-side in the same person? Clearly, I wasn't thinking rationally, because reason would surely rule out such a co-existence. What reading your letter has given me is a single word... "instinct".

If I was not consciously deciding to be either an

arsehole or a saint, then I must have been making decisions at a sub-conscious level—operating on instinct. As you have found out, that's what booby traps use to kill you. I've always liked looking at women's bits. At the age of five or six, I would show mine to Carol across the road and she would show me hers. No-one ever taught us this, it was pure instinct. We must have sensed it was naughty though, because we used to do it in her garden shed where no-one would find us. Magazines then took over. By my teens, if I'm honest, I wasn't really interested in girlfriends as such, I was only interested in female bodies. We used to discuss girls in terms of how far they would let you go. Whilst we admired those who got off with the pretty ones, was it worth it if they didn't let you go as far as the ugly ones did?

On the other hand, however, I also remember Mum's countless reminders about sharing my stuff with others, not lying, being kind when I didn't want to be, being polite to my friend's parents, and of course eating up all the food on my plate (because there are thousands of starving children in the world). Mum must have done a great job, because so many of these things she taught me now come naturally. I really don't have to think twice about being kind. And that's just it; these virtues that have become more or less instinctive had to be taught—second nature if you like, unlike my lustful desires that have caused me so much grief.

Aristotle was harping on about all this thousands of years ago. A virtuous man is one who is most truly human, and he argued that in order to be virtuous, one has to develop habits...a second nature. Virtuous behaviour is not a matter of theory, but of practice. By definition, it clashes with one's basic instinct in so many ways. Because we live in communities, we have to be able to assume that other people will behave in certain unselfish ways. Under the guidance of adults, the child must learn to put aside self-centred instinct and adopt the selfless habits that community living demands. I guess that's why all societies in the past have insisted that kids obey their parents!

So, I'm trying to work through this whole business of instinct and whether it's the product of nature or nurture. For instance, to what extent is conscience inbred or taught? Did the Iraqi soldiers trying to kill you guys have to retrain their consciences into accommodating the things they did to the Kuwaiti women? And, were these consciences ones that they had to learn in the first place at their mothers' knees? I once read about the commandant of a German concentration camp who would kiss his wife and kids every morning as he headed off to the office to oversee the extermination of thousands of wives and children. When I add all this to my own experiences, it makes me think that it would be impossible to rid the world of evil, because in that case, you'd have to kill everyone!

How depressing!

Shit...I had wanted to express something positive, but look what I've just written. Maybe there isn't anything positive to write? I'm grasping at straws here bro. But, then again, there was this Scot, David Hume, who was sceptical about pretty much everything from religion to science. He reckoned you couldn't be certain of anything. All you could do was assume that if things happened in a certain way in the past, they'd be likely to happen that way in the future. In fact, he really speaks into what you're going through because like you, he would agree that in theory, one could never be completely sure if a light switch was actually a light switch.

If we use past experiences to work out how things operate, we will always be taking a risk, because past experiences can never be more than a guide to the present. Even if you're poised on a cliff edge wondering whether or not to jump, you can't be absolutely sure that if you do jump, you'll plunge to the earth below. Every time you do anything, it is the first time you've done it 'this time', and what happened 'last time' can only suggest what will happen 'this time'. Although Hume was working this out in theory, not like you in a booby-trapped city, it still spooked him. When he got spooked, he used to invite some friends round, get the backgammon board out of the chest, pour the port, and enjoy life as it is.

So bro, it might just be that you could follow Hume's example and find something potent enough (gin and poker instead?) to temporarily transport your mind to a more mellow place.

Go Bro!

Cheers,

Pete

Pete,

You wouldn't believe just how timely your last letter was. Please believe that you waffling on about ancient philosophers has been a huge help to me. At times, my head has really been screwed up big style pretty much in the way you predicted at the end of your letter. But, just reading about it in the way you laid it out has helped me to step outside of myself and see where I've been travelling to. You'd make a great teacher, bro!

Actually, got no time to write anything more substantial — I'm squeezing this into a short break. I just wanted to thank you so much, and let you know how great your letter was.

Cheers,
Nick

Nick,

That's a bit of desperately needed good news. Mum's reaction to events in Kuwait is pretty much the only thing I've got at the moment. She needs me and this takes my mind off the fact that my shitty life has pretty much fallen apart. I hate those academic arseholes. They're so up themselves, it's unbelievable, and when I say 'they' I mean every last one of them. 'The Academy', as they refer to themselves, is a closed shop. They fancy themselves as open minded adventurers into the world of the "not yet but soon to be understood", but in truth, they're no different to any institutionalised bunch of humans. They protect their status by ensuring that you can only become an accredited academic if you play to their rules and lick their backsides. But hey, get it right and one day, you'll be able to enjoy having your backside licked, and why not your gonads whilst they're at it.

So, I'm reading up about Kierkegaard and his contribution to Western Philosophy. At first, it's really interesting—it is really speaking to me and my situation. But to start with, all I'm doing is reading about him, and, fairly soon, I begin to detect widely diverging views on what he thought. There is a mainstream opinion, but the dissenting voices are published in proper academic journals—one would assume they have a case to make. So, I set to and read some of his stuff, but my problems then begin. There's a shed load of it, and I've only got a week to write the essay. Not only that, but the way he writes means that you find yourself reading a single page over and over again. Even then, you don't always catch his drift. That's not all though, he liked to write under pseudonyms in order to adopt different personalities. So, when he wrote something, was it because that is what he actually thought? Oh, and one last problem — he wrote in Danish. Given my distinct lack of Danish, I have to read his work in translation.

So there I am in the tute, and Dr Bollocks is interrupting my reading to have a go at something I've written. I try to sustain my case, he's having none of it. I just flip. "How can I possibly know what the fuck Kierkegaard thought..." And with that, I just lay into him, and specifically, his academic arrogance. My choice of words is far from deferential, and I round it all off by calling him a wanker. Dr Bollocks rises to his feet and tells me to get out. Such language is not tolerated in learned establishments and I am to await a disciplinary action. I storm out, swearing as I go, dismissing him and the college as the cesspit of Calcutta. I've had it. I go back to my room and just sit there.

A note comes saying I have a hearing before the Provost in a fortnight's time—he's too fucking busy to see me any earlier. And so I sit in my room. I just sit there in my chair, surrounded by nothing but bare concrete walls. Right from the start, I considered the place not worth personalising, and I'm under warning from the college bursar for leaving it in a shit state. I could get on with preparing an essay I'm having to read at a seminar, but

I don't know where to start. I've done some research, but now all I can think is "What's the point?" Why do I have to keep on saying what others think when I can't ever know what they thought? And, if I have to say what I think, well...I haven't a fucking clue what I think. I'm feeling like a crack in my head is being prised apart and becoming a gaping chasm. It's dark, and there's no bottom in sight and I'm beginning to tumble into it. The crazy thing is that I know I'm tumbling into it, and although I feel somehow I could stop myself falling, I don't want to...

Everything is fucked. Everything I ever wanted has let me down. I had a dream life of sex on tap, and all it did was to reveal to me what a shit I am. And then I arrived in Oxford to read PPE, my other massive dream, but I've ended up sitting on a chair in the fucking prison cell College has put me in. All it has done is confirm what I had learnt in Majorca; nothing is what it is cracked up to be. When your two great dreams in life—the ones you've always believed in—come true, yet fail to deliver, where does that leave you? I just sat there.

I never attended the disciplinary. My cleaner apparently came into my room and found me sitting in my chair with shit oozing out of my trousers and a pool of piss around my feet. I'd been sitting there for two days. The letter telling me that I'd been sent down arrived in the post this morning. So here I am at home with Mum who, fortunately for me, is in such a state about you that she can't really focus on my plight. And, that's despite Dad who has just gone to hospital because of the fucking booze—probably for the last time.

I get away from here as much as I can, usually in Dad's car. I drive, I drive fast, to nowhere in particular. I like the fact that I don't know where I'll end up, the uncertainty of the journey. I want to get lost but somehow, I never quite manage it. Eventually, I find my way home.

Well, there you have it from your fucked up little bro.

Cheers,
Pete.

Hey little bro,

I want to tell you so much, but don't quite know where to start. As I sit here, I kind of think I have all the time in the world to ponder because I'm not sure you're going anywhere soon, and I'm certainly not. I visited you yesterday. Mum came and picked me up, and I was with you all afternoon. I sat in your room and looked at you. You looked so normal. I think that is what affected me the most. You looked absolutely ok…as if there was nothing wrong. I kept on thinking that you'd say something, even though I was told that it was really unlikely. Nevertheless, Mum wanted me to talk to you in case the sound of my voice triggered off something in your head and kick-started an area of your brain into some kind of activity. I did talk, Pete. I talked and talked and talked. All afternoon, I talked. I told you everything about Kuwait, and you looked at me all the time and I was desperately trying to work out if you were hearing anything?

The doctors say that your body was not too badly damaged in the crash. But, the blow to your head seems to have fucked up your brain. They reckon you're aware of what is going on around you, but that you can't communicate what you are thinking?

In the end, I had to return early from Kuwait because I completely lost it. In spite of reading what you wrote about Hume, I found that 'backgammon and port' didn't work for me. Trevor had left because he blamed himself for Kirstie—it was he who had persuaded her to stay on the job when she had desperately wanted to go home. He's in a bad way.

His Mrs is finding him hard work, but when I visited, it seemed to help. She's an amazing person. God knows where he'd be without her, and his kids help too.

Kirstie is receiving loads of treatment, you know, physio and all that stuff. They're working on artificial limbs which are way more advanced than ever before. Her man is completely dedicated to her, and it seems that she had the good sense not to tell him about us...I think she'll be okay.

I've been seeing a shrink and it's actually helped me... just as well since I had gotten to the point where life had almost become impossible. You mentioned instinct; well I had reached the place where I began instinctively to reject my instinct. I would look at an everyday object, say a doormat, but somehow, whilst the notion that it was a doormat hovered around, it would never land because it might just be a pressure pad wired to a detonator. I found myself surrounded by objects that were vaguely familiar, but no more. It was terrifying, but thanks to time, I'm beginning to get there. Whilst I know I'm a long way off, at least there is a flickering light where before there was none.

Dad's dead...am I upset? Don't know. But then what do I know? My mind feels pretty mechanical at the moment, and somehow detached from my emotions. I know he's dead —a fact—but I don't seem to feel anything as a result.

Mum has become amazingly strong. I actually think Dad dying has relieved her of the agony of having to love him. Whilst I think she feels guilty at the relief she's experiencing, she is in a completely different place. I think me being home and beginning to improve has helped her, that and the fact that even though your body isn't functioning, at least the doctors say you're not going to die any time. They see no reason that in time to come, you might not gradually regain mastery of your body. She is an amazing woman, and an enormous source of strength to me. She embodies hope, and I'm leeching on to her and sucking desperately in order to find something for myself to hope for. I think it's working because I've found that I'm hoping that you recover. So long as I can believe in Mum, I have hope, and so do you my little brother.

Cheers,

Nick

"Moral rules ought not to be such as to make instinctive happiness impossible."

— Bertrand Russell —

A Little Extra...

The original version of this story contained a sizeable section about John Locke and David Hume. A friend read it and objected to what he saw as a ruinously crass attempt to smuggle a block of teaching into a passably interesting story. As I read it through in the light of his comments, I too saw the classroom teacher spilling out in my prose. So I cut it, and lo an behold, as I did so, I discovered a far more significant theme emerging into the narrative. Notwithstanding this improvement, I have decided to append the chopped material just in case it is of interest–and because I spent quite a bit of time on it in the first place!

There was once an Englishman and a Scotsman—John Locke and David Hume. They were around in the 18th Century and doing a load of joined-up thinking at a time when men were becoming increasingly confident in science and its ability to offer up explanations.

Locke reckoned that there are two types of knowledge: *ideas* and *reflections*. Ideas are what our senses take on board and deliver to the mind that then processes this input in order to generate reflections. In this way, he linked reason to experience, and, in a sense, this is science at its most basic. We are, all of us, scientists—we experience something and use our reason to generate reflections. A young girl in a skirt is walking down a path, and, suddenly, she brushes past a plant and her shin starts to itch. Small pale lumps indicate where she is itching. She has to work out why her shin itches, and usually, with the help of a parent or friend, learns about nettles and how to recognise them. Several months on and she will have worked out that nettles can't sting you through thick jeans, but thin cotton trousers are a different matter. This is how most of us do science, though to be sure, most of us associate the word science with what we encounter at school in the laboratory. Here, the experiments we conduct facilitate in-depth study, and are simply careful recreations of naturally occurring events. Fable has it that an apple fell on Newton's head. He recreated the event in a laboratory in order to analyse what had happened. In due course, he would describe the laws that predict how rapidly an apple falls and in what direction. Newton was good at discovering natural laws, and his third law was pretty major. Nothing happens unless something causes it to happen, and everything that happens causes something else to happen. Thus we have 'cause and effect'...a law that stretches beyond the laboratory into the very soul of human history.

Back to Locke whose theory is called Empiricism. He implied that when trying to work out what's what, the most important information is that which someone has actually experienced happening. There would still be claimed events that strayed beyond the bounds of scientific logic, e.g. miracles. These instances would require faith to accept, and for Locke, such faith is dependent on the reliability of the one making the claim in the first place. So, a five year old girl claiming to have had a conversation with a fairy at the bottom of the garden is treated differently to a physicist claiming to have evidence of a single electron being in two different locations simultaneously.

Locke liked facts, and he like the way in which the human brain could process these facts and make sense of things. And in a sense, John Locke, the Englishman, laid the groundwork for David Hume, the Scot, to come along and cast a shadow of doubt over absolutely everything. He argued that it is impossible to predict the future with absolute certainty based simply on one's experience of past events. You watch your neighbour walking his dog. The dog runs off, the neighbour whistles, and the dog returns to his side. Every day, you see this happen without fail. Using your mind, you reason that the man whistling causes the dog to return to him. But one day, the man whistles and the dog doesn't come running. Clearly, the man whistling cannot be the cause of the dog returning. Now there's nothing untoward here, but suppose you decided to run an experiment on whether the new £1 coin would be an ideal coin to toss before the FA Cup final. You get a notebook and pen, and start tossing the coin and writing down the outcome of each toss. Much to your amazement, it keeps on coming down tails. No matter what you do, how you toss it, it always comes down tails. For over a hundred tosses, it's tails…five hundred tosses…a thousand tosses and a thousand tails. Whilst such an outcome is highly unlikely, it is possible. And, if it did happen, you might rightly conclude that you had proven 'scientifically' that this particular £1 coin always landed tails. After all, any experiment conducted a thousand times that yielded a constant outcome would be considered proof enough... except that on toss one thousand and one, it comes down heads.

So, Hume argued that all science can do is tell you what has happened in the past. He argued that, as a result, cause and effect couldn't exist, that you can't say that 'a' caused 'b'. All you can say is that, in your experience, when 'a' occurs, 'b' occurs afterwards. He wrote:

> *"'Tis not, therefore, reason, which is the guide of life, but custom. That alone determines the mind, in all instances, to suppose the future conformable to the past. However easy this step may seem, reason would never, to all eternity, be able to make it."* [7]

If this is the case, what is the point of conducting experiments? Why should one engage one's grey matter trying to identify relationships between events when one can never be sure that just because it's always happened like that in the past, it will happen like that in the future?

Hume was no fool. He actually realised the dark destination of this train of thought which is why he used to invite his friends round for backgammon and port. The French philosopher, Sartre, did explore the logical consequences in his novel, Nausea. The hero, Roquentin, becomes exhausted by the experience of forever having to live in the present as he finds himself increasingly abandoning his memory as a guide to the present. He has to rely solely on his sight and touch to make sense of his surroundings. He is in a room surrounded by objects that he refuses to allow his memory to identify. He looks at an object, and whilst the label 'seat' seems to hover above it momentarily, it refuses to land on the object itself. Roquentin finds himself surrounded by objects that are disturbingly familiar and yet unidentifiable.

---

7. David Hume, *Treatise of Human Nature*, I:III:12

The simple truth is that when someone says they don't believe in anything, they are almost certainly mistaken. There will be a whole load of things they do believe in, including, quite possibly, the fact that there is no God since this is a core belief that seems to encourage many people into erroneously claiming to be nihilists.

There is one final point worth considering though.

Hume's approach is known as Scepticism since he is denying the possibility of any kind of certainty, and challenging reason's ability to work out what's what. On the other hand, the whole point of Philosophy is to work out the answers to the big questions of life through the application of reason, rather than appealing to the metaphysical outpourings of religious people. In other words, Hume is undermining the value of reason, the basic principle of Philosophy, through the application of reason! He is logically working out that there's no point in logically working anything out.

Mmmmmm.

Sonja Kharoud

"This is My Truth Tell Me Yours"

— Manic Street Preachers —

Notwithstanding the fact that the bench she lay slumped on offered a glorious, panoramic view over Windermere, Sonja's state of mind was such that it went completely unnoticed. The deep waters of the lake reflected the bright azure of the sky in vain, and the sailing dinghies that flirted with each other singularly failed to catch her eye. Sonja Kharoud had not reckoned with ever being able to feel this wretched, not least because she thought she had plumbed the depths of despair barely a year earlier.

For the first 24 years of her life, she had been a largely content individual who enjoyed life within the boundaries that her mother had laid out for her. Some might have said that these boundaries were more constraining than they ought to have been, but they were those with which Sonja had been brought up. For her, they were as much a part of her life as might be the freedom to switch on the TV at whim to someone else. Indeed, watching television was one of the many restricted activities that Sonja had to live with. But, along with comparatively small amounts of pocket money, early bed times, church twice on a Sunday and a ban on Radio 1, she had just got on with it. She knew where she stood. Whilst from time to time, she had wondered what it might be like to have unfettered use of the telephone, she was too grateful to her mother to upset her by flouting her rules.

Her mother, Mary Kharoud, was a widow. Harman, her husband and Sonja's father, had killed himself when he could bear the pain no longer. He had driven to Batley in the early hours of the morning, parked outside his parents' house, connected a hose to the exhaust pipe and passed it through the passenger-side window. His final, deeply apologetic note simply said that death presented itself as the only way of bringing his torment to a close.

Harman's parents had been amongst the first of the Punjabis to arrive in Batley in the 1950's, and their cheap labour in the *Shoddy Mills* had postponed the mills' inevitable demise by a couple of decades. Harman had been born shortly after their arrival. Mary, on the other hand, was born into a family that had lived in Batley for several generations. Her parents were salt of the earth, Yorkshire born and bred, working class, and life-long Labour supporters.

Harman was a Muslim, and Mary was a member of the local Wesleyan Chapel. Nonetheless, she and Harman had fallen for each other as young school leavers working in the local mill. Yes, at first, they had just got on with getting to know each other, but as they grew to like each other, Mary slowly began to grasp the full enormity of what was happening. Harman had known from the outset that to have a relationship with a local girl would be disastrous, but drawn by Mary's pale beauty, he had initiated a conversation one lunch time. At the time, he had no intention of doing anything other than seeing if she would speak to him.

He had been surprised by her willingness to engage. Soon however, when it became obvious that she was as attracted to him as he was to her, he found himself incapable of pulling out of a deepening relationship, in spite of knowing where it would lead.

Mary and Harman both knew that their respective families would be furious, and so their burgeoning relationship was furtively played out. Perhaps it was this secrecy that saw it consummated early on, notwithstanding the fact that both had inherited a powerful instinct against having sex outside of wedlock. Mary was still shy of her eighteenth birthday, largely ignorant of the implications of sexual intercourse, and pregnant before she knew what the signs were. Realisation came towards the end of her initial trimester, after chatting to one of her friends at work. She entered a period of denial, but when she felt the first whisperings of the life in her womb, she took herself off to the doctor who confirmed her state and informed her parents. To cut a long story short (for Mary and Harman's story is simply a prequel that gains its significance as an essential aid to grasping why Sonja was feeling so wretched at the opening of this tale), Mary and Harman made the fateful decision to endure ostracism and headed off to nearby Bradford. Here, Harman found work that paid enough for them to afford the rent of a single room in the Manningham area of the city. Once in Bradford, they got married. It was with regret for both of them that God was absent from the registry office ceremony. Whilst their faiths were different, both had a firm conviction in the authority of the one God, and both desperately wanted his forgiveness for what they had done. They hoped that he would accept their decision to marry as a sign that they were sorry.

Life was hard. They were in the middle of an immigrant area where Mary's white skin was impossible to conceal, and Harman's family made sure that the young couple faced the acrimony of their neighbours. After six months, when Sonja was six weeks old, they were effectively forced out of their room. It was at this point that Harman had stolen a car from work and driven to Batley to end it all. Although in one sense, this was completely disastrous, it did result in some kind of solution to Mary's plight. Without Harman at her side, she was accepted back into her family home—even if she was regularly reminded that she was the prodigal daughter.

Mary found work in a solicitor's office as a receptionist, and over the next few years, worked her way into the heart of the firm through hard graft and her ability to organise. Consequently, her salary rose and she started to save. When Sonja was six and in school, Mary had enough for the deposit on a small terraced house and moved out of her family home.

Mary had not abandoned her faith and, if anything, it became more important to her. Almost as if to prove the genuine nature of her repentance, she organised her life, and that of her daughter's, very tightly around what she perceived to be an appropriate response to the Bible's call to live an upright and Godly life. It must be stated that Mary wanted to be a fair and loving mother, and in her own mind was determined to allow Sonja to make her own decisions as and when. Unfortunately, she was not very successful. Having a strong sense of right and wrong, she found it impossible to resist stepping in when Sonja strayed. If the delicate path she tried to tread was hard to make out, then an observer might have concluded that she was rarely on the path in the first place. But, there were very few observers.

Whilst her opinions were pretty inflexible, she did at least discuss them with her daughter. In this way, Sonja understood why her mother restricted her in ways that marked her out from her friends at school. From time to time, Mary would lift a restriction, either because she thought Sonja old enough, say, to schedule her own homework, or because, on the very rare occasion, Sonja persuaded her to change her mind. She often wondered how she would react if Sonja turned to her one day and said she no longer believed in God. It transpired, however, that this never happened. One thing was for sure though; Sonja would never be allowed to make the same mistake that had caused her mother so much grief.

For Sonja growing up, life came in two halves. At school, things could be tricky. In the late eighties, there were not a large number of Anglo-Asian youngsters in Batley—the Asians rarely married out. The Yorkshire kids thought she was a "Paki", and the Asian kids refused to look on her as one of them. It was therefore of huge significance that at home, she felt completely safe. Her mother felt wise and loving, and home supplied her with enough security to cope with the difficulties she faced at school. Indeed, her ability to cope meant that as the years wore on and she entered her teens, she had built up several good friendships with girls who, though she didn't recognise this, were drawn to her because she was so contentedly independent. Sonja was indeed becoming more and more attractive, but not in a physical sense. Although she did possess aspects of her mother's beauty, they were tempered by the very Punjabi nose that was her father's contribution to her appearance. Put simply, she was a person who was comfortable in her own skin. She had learnt how to follow her own distinctive course, without drawing attention to herself, and was respected by her peers for being a kind and loving person. At sixteen, she became one of the first girls to enter the sixth form at the hitherto boys-only grammar school, where she flourished. Her self-confidence underpinned her ability and industry. In her final year, she was made a prefect, and then became the first member of her family to go to university—Manchester—to read English. During her second year, Sonja's life took an interesting turn.

Sonja had joined the University Ten-Pin Bowling Club during her first term, largely because of the persuasive technique of a lively duo of bowling enthusiasts. It was something she had never done, but this particular pair had made it sound fun—the kind of society where she would be able to forge some friendships. Every Tuesday afternoon, thirty or so students would head off to the local alley and play three games for a much reduced fee—shoe hire included. Here began a comfortable relationship with a sport to which she found herself surprisingly well suited. At first, she couldn't believe how heavy the balls were, and her efforts to propel one of them at pace meant that the gutters regularly swallowed the ball well before it reached the pins. It didn't take her long to realise that accuracy was more important than power, and over the weeks, her scores improved. By the end of the first term, she regularly surpassed 100, and by the end of the year, she had once scored an very impressive 196. In fact, a failure to exceed 135 would leave her disappointed.

At the end of the year, Sonja had stood for club secretary, and had been elected nem. con. by a group of students who were now solidly her friends. Because of this, she was at the freshers' fair at the beginning of her second year, encouraging the new intake to try out bowling. Reg Oldham was one of the lads she persuaded to sign up. He was a pleasant looking eighteen year old who gave off all the signs of being shy and uncertain. Her warmth, born of her quest to get members for the club, had felt to him like a much sought after offer of friendship. Recognising that Reg's initial experience of bowling pretty much matched hers—in that he was trying to fling the balls down the lane with as much force as possible—Sonja made sure she was in his trio the following week.

So began their relationship.

It wasn't long before Sonja found herself attracted to Reg in a way she hadn't experienced before. Interestingly, his attraction lay not so much in his looks, which she admitted were growing on her, but in something that was far less tangible. Whilst Batley had boasted its fair share of fanciable lads, she had focused her efforts on meeting the grade demands of Manchester. That, combined with a respectful fear of her mother—who she knew would disapprove—meant that she hadn't allowed herself to think of boys in terms of boyfriends. She caught herself looking at Reg's mouth and wondering what it would be like to kiss him, or anyone else for that matter. Increasingly, she simply wanted to be with him. She started to seek him out on campus, and even sought a copy of his timetable in order to create apparently random encounters. Reg appeared grateful to have a friend, and though there was no hint that he was attracted to Sonja in that way, it fast became clear that the desire to spend time together was mutual. After a few months of this, Sonja became frustrated. She tried to flirt, but wasn't sure how to and so felt clumsy. In the end, on an early winter evening, whilst walking from one of the university canteens to the bus stop, she stopped, faced Reg, drew a breath and simply said that she really liked him. Whilst Reg fumbled around for a response, she lifted her lips to his and kissed him.

Thus was the inept, clumsy curtailment of the platonic phase of their friendship that was to contribute to the wretchedness that Sonja was experiencing on the bench overlooking Windermere.

Being uncertain of what they wanted to do upon graduation, both applied for postgraduate studies and were accepted. For the ensuing years, Reg and Sonja just kind of belonged to each other. Sexual intercourse never happened because Sonja's upbringing had always emphasised its restriction to the marital bed. Whilst she sometimes felt tempted to *go all the way*, Reg never pressed himself on her so it never happened.

Maybe it was Sonja's desire to experience sex with Reg that found her ever more eager to marry him, or maybe it was that she genuinely believed that she had found her man. But whatever the reason, the simple fact that their relationship had survived four years suggested a powerful mutual commitment. As Sonja became desperate to marry, Reg's indifference became more frustrating. In the end, she once again took the initiative. Somewhat unconventionally, she popped the question on the way home from seeing *A Midsummer Night's Dream* at the Royal Exchange Theatre—another carefully choreographed event.

Reg, typically, had been taken aback by Sonja's forthrightness.

The "I don't know but I'll think about it" answer left her in a very uncomfortable place for the next eight days. Reg did indeed carefully consider her proposition, and then, on Thursday evening, he called round after work with a dozen red roses and informed Sonja that he would be delighted to marry her. Along with the flowers, he had purchased a bottle of genuine champagne. For a pair who hardly ever drank, the exuberant haste with which they despatched the bottle led to a light headedness…that led to passionate kissing…that led to intimate caressing. Finally, amidst lustful groping, they consummated their relationship in a manner that felt entirely appropriate. Afterwards, Sonja lay back in her bed in a state of complete contentment—emotional, physical and spiritual. She bent her naked body around Reg's and rested her head on his chest. She loved the feel of his flesh, and was overtaken by a deep desire for him to stay the night—she wanted to wake up the next morning and see him lying there. "Let's go to sleep," she murmured quietly. At first, he seemed to accede to her request, but after fifteen minutes or so, he got out of bed and reached for his clothes. He apparently didn't want to sleep with her, and left apologising.

Sonja was disappointed that she was no longer wrapped around him, but this barely dampened her elation which was such that it dispelled any guilt she might have felt. In a weird sense, smashing through the most sacred of her mother's boundaries had been strangely liberating. The next morning, she was self-assured as she dialled her mother's number to make the call that would lead to the breaking off of her engagement.

Before Sonja could say anything, her mother had said,

"Sonja, I've something to tell you." Had she known what was to follow, she might have ended the phone call, but such an action wouldn't have changed anything. "Martin Cleary has left his wife and has moved in with me." As the words sank in, Sonja's legs threatened to give way.

"I know that…" her mother continued—what she went on to say, Sonja would never know. She dropped the receiver, and stared at it on the floor as though it was a hissing viper.

Martin Cleary was the minister of their church back in Batley, and unknown to anyone, had been enjoying the pleasures of Sonja's mother for the past two and a half years. The monstrous agony of guilt both had felt after their first time had delayed their second session for six weeks, but no-one had found out, so it happened again. As the months passed, the gap between their trysts became shorter, and the guilt a little less, until the time came when Martin no longer wished to be apart from Mary. He had told his wife that he was leaving her, moved in with Mary, and resigned from his post in the church.

For several weeks, Sonja ignored her mother's attempts to get in touch. She hastily replaced the receiver if she heard her mother's voice, and threw away envelopes addressed in her script. Initially, her feelings had been all over the place, but were now settling down into a deep anger at being betrayed. She had revisited all the privations that had been imposed on her, which she had always been able to accept, but the discovery of her mother's abominable sin had changed everything. There had been a brief period when a degree of empathy assuaged her anger, empathy with a woman who had struggled on her own, and who perhaps deserved the love of a man. But not this way, not by wrenching a man from his wife and family. Her empathy was short lived and petered out, leaving only the anger.

Although she didn't realise it at the time, her anger had also grown out of the fact that her mother's actions had obliterated the person who she had admired almost to the point of worship. She had never considered her mother to be anything other than a paragon of virtue. It was this virtue, one of the givens in Sonja's life, and which had been integral to her sense of security, that now lay smashed. She no longer had anyone to look up to, no one by whose example she could measure her own life. Most cruel of all though, was that this most unexpected of betrayals caused her to question her relationship with Reg in a way that took her by surprise.

Sonja remembered asking her mum if she loved God more than she loved her. Mary had been very assured; she did indeed love God more than she loved her daughter, but this was a good thing. Sonja could be certain that she would love her to the end because that is what God wants parents to do. Some people stop loving their children, but for a Christian, someone who loves God, this is forbidden. Sonja had believed this wholeheartedly. How wrong she had been. Her mother's actions clearly exposed a lack of love for God, and, for that matter, her—it was hard to imagine that someone who loved you could knowingly apply this much pain to your life. And if her belief in her mum's love for her had been mistaken, then what chance was there of ever knowing if Reg loved her?

How could one ever be certain of another's love for them? A line from one of Shakespeare's sonnets wouldn't leave her head: "Love is not love which alters when it alteration finds."

She remembered how it had struck her when she had first read it during her final year. This truth had instantly been applied to the consistency of her mother's love, a love that had now been found wanting. How could she be sure that Reg really did love her? And, if she couldn't be sure, was marriage a risk she could take? She wondered how Mrs Cleary and the Cleary boys were feeling.

One thing she was sure of though was that she loved Reg… or did she? When she thought about it, hadn't she pursued Reg and made all the moves? Hadn't she done her level best to get him? It had even been her who had proposed to him, and it had taken him eight days to respond. Actually, far from loving, hadn't she been hugely selfish throughout the whole of their relationship? She had wanted him, but had she ever paused to consider whether he wanted her? How unloving could one be? Can it ever be right to persuade someone that they freely want something that they had never desired in the first place?

Ever since her mother had shattered her elation, Reg had been amazing, totally given to helping her. Perhaps he simply felt sorry for her? And, how cruel that this had happened just as she had at last found herself completely set free from all inhibitions and worries, so as to feel a pure sense of utter well-being. On a couple of occasions, her unabating antagonism towards her mother had got to Reg, and he had said some angry words. Once, he had even walked out, but was back half an hour later with some flowers of reconciliation and they had made love. That this had made her feel better simply confirmed that she was using him. She clearly couldn't love him because she was being so selfish.

Eight weeks after Sonja had asked Reg to marry her, she

ended the relationship. She had prepared what she was going to say, and had accurately predicted Reg's horrified response. Firm and reasonable rebuttals to his increasingly desperate objections were also prepared in advance. It would be better, she had finally stated, if they didn't see each other for a bit. With that, she had turned about and walked confidently away from what was by now a tearful, forlorn figure. Sonja managed to hold it together until she was out of sight, but it had been a close run thing.

As a matter of expediency, she informed her Masters supervisor that she was terminating her studies forthwith, and applied to be a volunteer with an aid charity that worked amongst the poor in South America. She had been involved with the charity ever since she was sixteen, when her church was visited by a group of its people—two of whom had been Bolivian. Their situation back home had moved her and, before leaving for university, she had got involved in fund raising for them. Now, finally, an opportunity to volunteer had arisen, and she hoped to work in Bolivia under their authority. In fact, she ended up in Peru, in Puno, on the banks of Lake Titicaca. Her initial disappointment evaporated rapidly in the face of the squalor she encountered. The privation of so many local people also offered plenty of distraction from her issues back home. Whilst she was certainly not particularly happy deep down, she nevertheless derived some degree of genuine contentment from the work she was engaged in.

Why it was almost twelve months before she visited the small community on the Island of Taquile, she wasn't sure, but now that she was about to go home on furlough, she decided to follow the tourist trail. Two days before her departure, she boarded a somewhat beat up motorboat that chugged its way out to the island. Over her time in Puno, she had heard about this island and its tightly knit community of 1500 or so souls. They were known to keep to themselves, and her visit confirmed what she had read. It was obvious to even the casual tourist that the life of a Taquilean was pretty much a given from the moment of birth. With hardly any space to deviate from a clearly defined straight and narrow, their elaborate clothes and regular celebrations in the square were simply for the entertainment of the tourists—their sole source of income. The men knitted, the boys learnt how to knit, and the women did pretty much everything else, including sitting at their husband's feet in public. 'Freedom' might be just a boat ride away in the port of Puno but most eschewed this opportunity. Those who did pursue it usually returned after a few years of experiencing its oppressive reality. At first, Sonja wondered why this should be since it was clear that choice on Taquile was seriously restricted—she suspected that even marriages were arranged. That evening, back in the hostel which she helped run for a collection of young women and their children, she found herself focusing on the word 'choice'. She thought of the Taquileans, and she thought also of the choices she had made of late.

Thus began the final phase of Sonja's journey to the Lake District bench, where she now sits in serious mental anguish. She's staying with a family who are members of the church in Kendall that she's been with over the weekend on behalf of her charity. It's a bright sunny Monday morning and, now that the business of the weekend is over, she can no longer prevent the pain from crushing her completely. It is immaterial that her physical body is not its source; the pain has sought out every cubic centimetre of her being. Back in Puno, she had decided that life is about choices, but that no-one can ever be certain of any outcome. But more than that, certainty is a dangerous notion that is more than capable of generating great suffering. So, whilst it might just be that an *absolute truth* exists, the fact that you can't be certain of what it is means that it might as well not exist in the first place. You end up in the same place as the Taquile teenager; either choose to submit to a shared version of the truth adopted by your community, or establish your own by making a different series of choices.

If Sonja's journey to her next choice had taken a lifetime, it took only an instant to make. In two days' time, she was returning home and was going to go to Reg and tell him what an idiot she had been. She would once again ask him to marry her. Knowing Reg as she did, she was sure he would say yes—even if it might take him a few days to come to the decision for himself.

She phoned him from the airport. The fact that there was no answer when she rang was not a problem; he was often out. The first awkward moment arrived when she rang an hour later and the phone was answered by someone other than Reg. Apparently, he had left Manchester. The person living in his flat didn't have a new phone number, just his forwarding address which was care of the Maths Department at Bristol University. No matter, why shouldn't he have moved? The fact that they hadn't kept in touch since the break-up meant that there was no way she could have known. She had driven the car the charity had lent her down the motorway to Bristol, rehearsing over and again the words she would say.

This was indeed a moment of excitement; things could finally be put back to how they were. She recalled the warmth of their friendship, and relived how they had started out. She smiled at the ridiculous circumstances of their first kiss, and dwelt on the day Reg had said yes—especially the feeling of pure joy that had lit up her soul in the aftermath of making love. She could do nothing about the thrill she felt as she found the Maths department and was directed to the space where Reg's desk was located. At last, she was going to have what she had always wanted.

Sonja entered a large work space and spotted his desk. Whilst Reg wasn't there, its clutter made it clear that he was somewhere in the department. Approaching the desk, she surveyed its contents, and spotted the plain perspex frame and its photograph…of a woman. On closer inspection, she appeared ordinary looking and somewhat overweight. Panic welled up as she began to run through the various possibilities. Indeed, the tendrils of hope she was now clinging to had become pathetically fragile. She stood motionless for a while as the panic began to turn to anguish.

"Hello?" enquired a familiar voice from over her shoulder.

She turned round, and even before she looked at his face, she sought out his left hand and spotted the gold band on his finger. Her personal tragedy was confirmed.

"What are *you* doing here?" queried Reg in astonishment.

The words were lost.

Sonja fled across the room and ran out of the building. She headed off in a direction that was significant only in as much as it increased the distance between herself and Reg…and this

Windermere bench was a long way from Bristol.

This is my truth, tell me yours…

The title of a Manic Street Preachers' album floated around in her head. She contemplated the mysterious disappearance of their guitarist, whose car was found abandoned one night by the Severn Bridge. Might she follow suit? She was fed up with being Sonja Kharoud. Speaking about her charity's work to the Christians in Kendall had been hard. Because of her pain, she had disconnected herself from the person who was running through the slide show, and had followed the script to the letter. Afterwards, she couldn't get out of her mind the futility of it all. She had spent a year and more in Puno. Why? To serve Jesus, or to make herself feel good? Hadn't she in fact simply fled—to an isolated, god-forsaken corner of the globe—in order to fill her life with the pain and suffering of other people as a way of escaping her total uncertainty about everything?

And this was where she was on the bench. She had been trying to do God's work, but which god? What god?

Christ?

Why was she a Christian? Had she chosen to be one? Had she ever made that choice in the first place, or had her mother's influence extended to the God question? The significance of election suddenly erupted in her head. Election—the idea that God arbitrarily calls people to become his disciples—effectively removes the privilege of choice. Without choice, there can't be freewill. Furthermore, the fact that *God* is *Love* had, over the years, become something she had ceased to question, but it was now unravelling for it was clearly ridiculous. A God who 'calls' people cannot possibly expect these people to love him, because love that is not freely given cannot, by its very definition, be love.

Sonja realised that she had some more choices to make.

Could she live with the paradox of the simultaneous existence of Election and Freewill, or did their mutual exclusivity eliminate *God is Love*? But then, can God ever be understood? And if he were understood, would he still be God?

And of course, if it has to be freely given, what is love in the first place? If it depends on the giver, the one who loves, does this mean that love becomes nothing more than what the lover thinks it is?

If this is the case, how can anyone ever know if they are loved according to their own personal definition? Love doesn't just become a meaningless concept, it becomes the chief source of suffering for the whole of humanity. The word used to describe the ideal human relationship seemed to conceal the fact, and disastrously so, that there is absolutely no possibility of any consensus as to its meaning. It struck her that when Reg had said "I love you", she actually had no certainty as to his intention. Nevertheless, she unthinkingly applied her own understanding to the phrase and rejoiced—maybe others would have run a mile.

But some woman had not run a mile.

Anger bubbled up inside her as she considered the length of time it had taken for Reg to find another woman and to marry her. It had taken her literally years to get engaged to Reg, and some woman had now achieved it, and more, in barely twelve months. How come this woman was so much better than she was? How had she managed to get him to marry her so quickly?

But hang on. Hadn't Reg agreed to marry her first? She had totally screwed up. She'd had it all and thrown it away in a moment of madness. Every loving moment of their relationship now congregated in her heart and the ensuing jealousy rent it asunder. Suddenly, she found herself urgently needing to deflect some of the blame—to find, if possible, some explanation for her lunatic actions of a year earlier. As she searched around, 'love' came to the fore and refused to go away, and without any conscious effort on her part, 'God' popped up as well, and she was back where she started.

God and Love… if God is Love, and Love is merely a personal concept and not a real thing, then surely God can't be real either? In fact, if you spin it round, get rid of God and you can get rid of Love as well.

Could God's existence be dependent on an individual's decision to believe or not?

What would be the consequences of deciding that there is no God?

But then, how could the existence of anyone or anything be dependent on an individual's decision to believe in its existence or not? Either God existed, and with him Love, or neither existed. Which was it to be?

And then it hit her. In the Bible, Sonja had always known that God had chosen Abraham, had chosen the Jews, and in fact pretty much every major figure in the Old Testament. In the New Testament, Jesus had chosen his disciples, called them by name. He had even personally interrupted Paul, on his way to persecute Christians in Damascus, in order to call him. This latter story had always vexed her because it implied that Paul never had a choice, but now she was looking at it in another way.

The fact that God chose you meant that your faith did not solely rely on your decision as to whether to believe in God or not, but also on the fact that God chose you. God had to exist to choose you. That wretched paradox—Freewill and Election! Without Freewill, there can be no Love, but without Election, the existence of God—and therefore Love—is subject to ones personal choice. Perhaps the two could co-exist. Why can't there be paradoxes? Not only that, but this business of Love, and whether or not there can be a definitive definition of Love, finds itself being drawn towards the person of Jesus. If God is Love, and if Jesus is the man who is God, then in Jesus rests all that one can ever need to know about the true nature of Love.

Sonja felt the pain receding, and with these thoughts filling her head, she found herself able to think about the coming week.

"This is My Truth Tell Me Yours"

— Manic Street Preachers —

Author's note

Once I get into a tale, I tend to find that it flows. From time to time, it's almost as though I am no longer engaging with the story at a conscious level. Sonja's reflections as she looks out over

Windermere are an example of this. I have frequently revisited the text since I first typed it, because I find it somewhat tricky. In a sense, it seems to flow. The lines of argument feel consistent when you read it through, but when you get to the end, there's a niggle that wonders whether you did actually understand it. You go back and reread it, and this is where the difficulties start to emerge. As you dig into the prose, you find yourself becoming a bit confused. The deeper you dig, the more confusing it gets. I think this is because, at the end of the day, the more profound issues in life seem to actively resist attempts to neatly summarise them. I've made up this story to try to describe what Existentialism is. I suspect that it is as they say; three philosophers would offer four different understandings! Maybe this is why I tell stories…

Philosophy, like life itself, is a dialectical process. By this, I mean that from time to time, one's beliefs are challenged by one's experiences. When this happens, a dialogue opens up as you try to work out why it is that what you have experienced doesn't fit in with your beliefs. Very often, this arises out of suffering, and the pain of suffering can make this questioning very distressing. Let me offer you a real example.

In his autobiography, William Barclay, a New Testament theologian and prolific writer from the last century, tells the tragedy of losing his 21-year-old daughter and her fiancé. They drowned in a boating accident. He wrote, "God did not stop that accident at sea, but he did still the storm in my own heart so that somehow my wife and I came through that terrible time still on our own two feet." Notwithstanding this, because he had witnessed the drowning, and had prayed for God to save them, he concluded that God didn't interfere in the natural functioning of the world. After all, if this were not the case, he most certainly would have intervened. A strong argument can be made for the fact that this unimaginably painful experience had a profound impact on his subsequent theology. When dealing with New Testament accounts of miracles, he regularly offered alternative 'natural' explanations in order to escape the conclusion that God had thus interfered.

Therefore, and given that, by and large, a philosophical dialogue is a very personal one, I decided that making up stories —occasionally based on an episode in the life of a key figure—is a fair way of introducing an understanding of a philosophical idea. Many of you will doubtless have recognised that Sonja Kharoud bears a dim resemblance to Soren Kierkegaard, and that Reg Oldham and Regine Olsen are similarly alike. What I have written might be a million miles from their story, and who will ever know, but I enjoyed writing it. And, in doing so, felt that I gained an insight into the slippery concept that is Existentialism.

That's what I'm trying to do; I'm offering a way into these matters that is as much experiential as rational. I'm inviting you to enter into the thoughts and emotions of Sonja, hoping that by doing so, you might get a picture of Existentialism that, for some, may be more helpful than a textbook description. Perhaps more importantly though, telling a story is a gracious act that offers the listener the space to react subjectively, for the impact of a story has as much to do with the heart of the listener, as the skill of the teller.

The Tap

"There are no facts, simply interpretations"

— Friedrich Nietzsche —

Every twenty five rounds, you tap the handle of the weapon with the open palm of your left hand to adjust its point of aim by a quarter of a degree. In this way, out at 2000 yards, you've shifted the impact area of your bullets to the left by 25 feet. When the barrel hits the pre-positioned stake, you then tap the handle with the palm of your right hand, and the point of aim traverses back whence it came. It takes time to master the technique, to sense when twenty five rounds have been fired, but the regular beat of the gun offers up a rhythm that becomes a part of you. Once you've learnt to tap the handle with just the right amount of force, you have it, and it never leaves you. As the weeks and months pass, you make effective your lethal intent with an instinctive precision that doesn't require conscious consent. This is crucial if one wishes to wake up the following morning and carry on as before. In truth, firing out to 2000 yards is the easy part, because at that range, there is no way that you can see your impact on the enemy. At any rate, one's point of aim is merely an inanimate feature of enemy held territory—a prominent tree, a small hillock, or a ruined building. No, the soul searching stuff is when you are in the line and the enemy infantry have emerged from their trench and are making their way towards you.

If you are in a prepared position, you are shielded from enemy gun fire by solid sand-bags—you peer out of an aperture that is small enough to make it unlikely that you'll be hit. And so the number two feeds the tongue of the canvas belt into the breech. You cock the weapon twice and pull the trigger. This time, you see the impact of your actions. Determinedly advancing figures suddenly fold and fall as you traverse the gun from left to right. 'Figures' is a good word to use; it half disguises the reality of sons and brothers, fathers and husbands, indiscriminately being wrecked by your bullets. You tell yourself that they're being wounded rather than killed, that you're giving them all a 'blighty' that will see them returned home to convalesce. Whatever is the case though, you're getting them out of the hell that you yourself are trapped in. Sometimes, you actually find yourself envying the ones you kill because as they say, the only man for whom war is no more is the dead man.

Eighteen months earlier, I had stroked the barrel of a Vickers machine gun that was perfect in every regard. It was brand new, and we had carefully extracted it from its box and peeled away the lightly oiled brown paper that was designed to stop it rusting—boy did it smell of oil, rifle oil. I was as excited as an eighteen year old could possibly be. At that instant, I had thought of my father who was dead set against the war. Once again, I questioned his patriotism. His experiences whilst serving under Lord Kitchener in the Sudan were surely insufficient grounds for his pacifism.

Maurice, my father, had married his brother's sweetheart a couple of years after his brother had been killed at the Battle of

Omdurman. Although the British had been well outnumbered by the Mahdi's army, the battle was a one-sided massacre. Modern artillery and machine guns ripped down thousands of the Mahdi's men, none of whom got closer than 50 yards to the British Force. The brothers had been serving with the Lancers who charged an enemy position and had suddenly found themselves fighting over 2,000 hitherto concealed enemy troops. A brief but bitter struggle had ensued. After extracting themselves from the ambush, the regiment reformed and discovered my uncle was among the missing. Someone had seen him shot off his mount and was pretty sure he was dead, a fact that was confirmed by a search after the battle. Dad was distraught. If it wasn't enough that British deaths had numbered well under a hundred, he had promised his tearful mother, as they had embarked the troopship in Southampton, that he would look after his younger brother, Joe. He had not only failed in this, but had survived to bear the guilt of being able to tell the tale.

Marjorie, my mother, was completely shattered. She had been looking forward to a promised wedding even though she had not been formally proposed to. Distraught, she was drawn to the other woman who was sharing her grief, my grandmother, and they comforted each other. Through observing their distress, the span of my father's guilt came to include the misery he had caused her. Wanting to assuage it, he decided he would marry her. He proposed, she accepted, and so my mother joined the family after all. In fact, my parents were very happy together.

When war broke out, the men of Britain enthusiastically formed lines at recruiting offices. Whilst my father was borderline young enough to sign up, especially given his previous service, he had no desire to fight. He played his hand shrewdly, and was the foreman at a forge churning out thousands of rivets for all manner of military items.

But I wanted to join up. I wanted to fight for my King. I'm British, and as my father and his comrades had proved over the preceding two hundred years, we were the most powerful nation in the world. I had never quite understood my parents' resentment of the victory which we had won at Omdurman, nor their anger over the death of my uncle who had died for Queen and Country. Upset, yes, but surely mixed with pride. Nations do not become 'Great' without their menfolk being prepared to lay down their lives in battle. Such noble actions had given Great Britain its Great Empire, and being a Great nation brings Great responsibilities. So, if an evil nation decides to trample over its tiny neutral neighbour, then it needs to be taught a lesson. That was precisely the call to arms that I found irresistible.

I was only sixteen when war was declared, and I was terrified that it would be over before I could join up because the minimum age was eighteen. I was big for my age, with a dark complexion, and already had hair growing on my chin. However, I never managed to outmanoeuvre my parents who successfully prevented me from enlisting before my eighteenth. By the time I was eighteen, rising casualties had dampened my ardour, but I needn't have bothered because I was conscripted soon after. Because of my height—just under six foot—I found myself drafted into the Guards Machine Gun Regiment. My training began.

The fighting that kicked off in March 1918 consisted of a whole string of attacks by the Germans, which, for a long time, seemed to be taking them to victory. God knows how many men were killed. I dare not think how many of them I killed, but it must have been hundreds—maybe a thousand, or more even. A greater question is how on earth I managed to come through it all unscathed? As a machine gunner, you expect to be able to keep the enemy at arms length, but at one point, we were attacked from the rear. It got frantic and I've now looked into the eyes of a man as I killed him. When they are a hundred yards off, or even fifty, they are remote—even at ten yards, which happens, they are little more than figures. But when you get a face-full of fetid breath that stinks of rotting teeth, the figure becomes a man, a human being. As your knife sinks into his chest, you find yourself physically connected to him. You see the pain in his eyes and notice, in that moment of extreme passion, that he's got a forehead full of adolescent spots. When he slumps back into the earth, looks at you, and bursts into tears, you feel an outrageously painful compassion for this teenager you had determined to kill just thirty seconds earlier.

I didn't see him die—and maybe he didn't; perhaps he was rescued—because I was intent on staying alive, and this meant getting out of it. As I looked around, I realised that I was the only uninjured member of the gun team. We had been down to just three by this stage, but whilst Trevor was now clearly dead, Ken was still breathing. Across his midriff a deep crimson stain was visible, and the spreading had reached down his battle dress to his trousers. His hands were vainly attempting to stem the flow of blood from a sizeable gash. He had stopped shrieking though, and was now moaning softly.

I couldn't find my field dressing, even though I had no

recollection of using it, and I couldn't find Ken's either. Originally a weaver from Burnley, he was the old man of the team. One of his sons had brought it a couple of months back and since then, he had withdrawn into himself and had carried out his duties as though he was no longer inhabiting his body.

I considered lifting him onto my shoulders, but given the location of his injury, how could I? So, I scooped him up into my arms and started out. But, which direction to head in? The Germans had come upon us from behind, so I headed roughly south. This led me in a direction parallel to the frontline —even if the speed of the German advance had all but eliminated such a notion. After just a few hundred yards, my arms were killing me to the point where I could no longer, literally no longer, hold his weight.

I put him down and rested. I told him everything would be all right, but, whether he took anything in, I'll never know. I lifted him to carry on, but my arms once again gave out after a hundred yards or so. I knew there was no way I would be able to continue, but I felt compelled. This was my comrade, my friend. This was Ken who had a wife who had already lost a son, and I knew from my grandmother what this must have done to her.

After a short rest, I tried again, but was quickly done in. I placed him in a comfortable position and left. I said I was off to fetch stretcher bearers, and that they'd have him out in no time. In truth though, he had been bleeding like a stuck pig; I reckoned he had little time left. Did Ken die? I'm ashamed to say that, to this day, I don't know. He was recorded as 'Missing in Action,' and after the war, I never tried to find out.

Within minutes of moving off, I bumped into a group of

Frenchies. At first, their unfamiliar uniforms and foreign words confused me, but it took no time for us to work out what was what. I did try to ask for stretcher bearers but they didn't understand. At any rate, they were also cut off. We set out together, and after a night in the open, hit the main French force early next morning. Somehow, I had managed to shove Ken into some dark recess of my mind, and leave him there. From time to time, he emerges to confront me. He's still there…I think.

I was with the Frenchies for a couple of days, until matters sorted themselves out, and I was able to return to my own people—not that many of us were left. My brief spell with the French had a massive impact on me. There was just one bloke, by the name of Pierre Semard, who could speak good English. Whilst chatting, he opened my eyes to a way of looking at the war that had never occurred to me.

At the outset, I was astonished to discover that, a year earlier, there had been a major mutiny in the French Army. Their spring offensive had gone badly wrong and the soldiers were fed up. Deadly work and dreadful living conditions, combined with practically no leave, had led to men refusing to attack. Units had marched back out of the line, and whole regiments had refused to go up to the front. Thousands of men had been involved. The French generals, amazingly, had managed to keep it a secret. But, because the soldiers generally respected their junior officers, with whom they shared their lives, the events of the Eastern Front—where the Russian Army had revolted en masse—were not repeated in France. Many were sentenced to death, but few were actually executed. Instead, the soldiers got their leave and returned to the business of driving the German Army out of their Homeland.

Pierre, however, had not been pacified. He had instead woken up to the fact that hundreds of thousands of men were being killed as a result of the orders of just a few men. A few men, that is, who were getting it disastrously wrong. Not only that, but they were conducting the war from the safety of fancy chateaux a safe distance from the front line. French, German, British or Russian, it didn't matter; it was the same everywhere. The rich elite from the different nations had fallen out with each other, and were sending the working classes to their deaths in order to sort out their differences. In Russia, the working classes had had enough, and had taken control of their country. Pierre had tried to persuade his comrades to join him in following suit, but had failed. They were too exhausted. They lacked the energy to do anything other than concentrate on getting through the next hour unscathed. Fed up with his compatriots, who were fed up with him, he had spent his time with me, and I found him inspiring. I had never heard anything like it, and it made complete sense.

Why were we fighting this war? Because Europe's ruling classes had been vying with each other to be in command of the most powerful nation of all. Heavy industries had boomed, and technical advances had driven in a direction that had benefited the wealthy elite at the expense of the poor. Festering slums had been built to supply the factories with labour at the same rate as mansions had sprung up to house their owners. The poor had been fed a diet of patriotic rubbish that assured them that they were members of the greatest nation on earth. And it was working. It is a wicked scandal that the lives of the poor were being sacrificed to sustain the privileges of the few. But, accompanying this was a sad irony. Leading the poor to their deaths were the sons of the elite. They were dying at a more frightening rate than their men, and all to preserve the privileged life that they themselves would never enjoy.

So the Crown Prince of the has-been Austro-Hungarian Empire was assassinated by a Serb patriot in Sarajevo. Within a few weeks, German and British troops were killing each other as France was invaded through neutral Belgium, and all because Germany was afraid of Russia. Has there ever been a more ridiculous trigger for a conflict? But then, with hindsight, this was a war that was bound to happen some day. Moreover, we, the German, British and French peoples, just couldn't wait to get stuck into each other on the battlefield. Oh the power of lies. All of us, myself included, wanted to prove once and for all that we belonged to the greatest nation on earth. Now, at last, we had the opportunity to do so.

Unfortunately, no one had reckoned with the impact of a Swedish industrial chemist.

Dynamite is an amazing creation. It's an explosive compound that is solid, unlike gunpowder, and stable, unlike nitro-glycerine. That Alfred Nobel intended it for use in mining and quarrying is beside the point. It was a marvellous gift to armies everywhere. Over time, it was refined into cordite, the explosive used in bullets and shells. Before Nobel, 600 men, well trained, might fire three musket volleys a minute. After Nobel, four six-man teams, each with a Vickers, could more than match this fire power. Artillery also gained a fresh destructiveness, and as a result, warfare had, just like everything else, been industrialised. The rich weapon factory owners filled their pockets. Their products also provided big profits for those who sold the shovels that dug the graves beneath the white wooden crosses that surrounded the flattened villages of Belgium.

Anyway, shortly after finding my battalion, I found myself wandering through the streets of a small Belgian town called Poperinge. There, I came across a building with a sign that named it 'TOC H'. I think I'd heard of it, but never knew what it was—beyond the fact that it was a base for Army Chaplains. Initially, I had no desire to do anything other than walk past, but I spied an instruction written over the door: 'Abandon all rank ye who enter here.' Could this be anything other than an example of wishful thinking? I found myself wanting to go in, if only to sate my curiosity. On doing so, I discovered that yes, as far as one could tell, it was a place where all men were equal. I couldn't believe that such a place was possible. Whilst it was often obvious from an individual's demeanour what rank he held, it was, nevertheless, Christian names all round. I beheld an atmosphere such that I had yet to encounter since joining up. Indeed, I had never really encountered such fellowship before in my life. I felt inspired, even exhilarated. Here was a beam of light sneaking its way into the black tunnel of inhuman carnage that was driven largely by the class system. I found myself spending as much time as I could there, and whilst the God aspect was always interesting, it was never compelling. You didn't need to be a God-botherer to recognise that this approach to human relationships was infinitely preferable to that which existed in the fields beyond the walls of this amazing house.

After the war, I returned home and got involved in the

TOC H movement that had emerged from this classless experiment in Poperinge. At first, it was great fun. There was purpose, a direction, and a fantastic burst of energy. Those of us who had marched home in one piece desperately wanted to do something…anything…that would ensure no repetition for future generations. TOC H was the vehicle that attracted our attention as the one that could make this happen. All over the country, TOC H's were being built and communities set up aimed at pursuing the dream of a classless society. Perhaps it was the challenge of getting everything established that meant I failed to recognise the reality of post war Britain. I think the moment I realised all our efforts were in vain was when Woodbine Willie died.

The Reverend Geoffrey Studdart Kennedy was the most famous army chaplain of all. He had been the darling of the private soldier, not least because of the endless supply of Woodbine cigarettes that he handed out as he chatted with them. He wrote poetry that was widely read throughout the country, but he was hated by the Generals because he ignored rank and privilege. As a result, he was loved all the more by the lads. After the war, he quite literally worked himself to death, championing the poor for the Industrial Society. When his body was returned from Liverpool to Worcester, where his funeral was to take place in the cathedral, thousands upon thousands of ordinary people came out to pay their respects in the towns along the route. At the actual service, however, the elite emerged to sit in the front rows. It dawned on me that no number of TOC H's could ever unseat the elite of Britain who had, by this time, convinced us that it was they who had led us to victory. And so, my mind returned to my conversations with Pierre Semard which had all this time lain dormant.

Semard had made an impact on me; he had undermined the very way I looked at the world. I had developed a powerful urge to disconnect myself from the war that he had persuaded me was one huge, vain, catastrophic folly. I came close to deserting, but two things had stopped me. My TOC H encounter was one, but the more insistent reason was that, on my return to my company, I was made a lance corporal. Having charge over others, I found I couldn't abandon this responsibility of care—the memory of Ken goaded me. By the war's end, I was a sergeant—crazy at twenty, but that's how it was in those times. I even had a medal for bravery, though in truth, all I had done was get my men out of a sticky situation.

And so, a dozen years on, I fetched the medal out of the drawer where I kept it. All I could see was the King's head on it, a symbol of all that was rancid in our nation. I flung it into the fireplace and watched the ribbon catch light and burn. Millions had been killed, but nothing had changed. Unless something was done, it would only be a matter of time before we would be killing each other in another bloody war.

I'd occasionally come across the Communist Party during my work with TOC H. Reading about the amazing way in which the Russian working classes had liberated themselves from their ruling elite, I just knew we had to do the same in Britain. I sought out my local group and joined. I was not in the least surprised to discover that Semard was a leading light in the French Communist Party. I recalled afresh our conversations back in those terrifying days of 1918, and saw clearly that armed struggle was in fact the only way forward. TOC H had got it all wrong. As for poor, tragic Woodbine Willie, all that his efforts had produced was his premature death and a widow with young kids.

British history had proven lethal. Talk of the Empire had given us a misplaced sense of dominance, and because we had suffered fewer casualties than the Germans, our sense of global pre-eminence had grown. We simply had to forget our past—it was the only way of moving forward. We had to focus on the future. Instead of risking our lives and killing others for the lies of the past, we needed to risk our lives and be prepared to kill for the egalitarian society of the future. Yes, the choicest prize was now all that the Soviet Union dangled before our eyes. For sure, people had killed and been killed in their revolution, but how else was power ever going to be wrested from the ruling classes? This would ultimately have to happen here.

Marx had said that Religion was the opiate of the working classes, and now I understood what he meant. The rich ruled with impunity and enjoyed lavish material benefits at the expense of the poor. Why, in Britain, did we put up with this? After all, we outnumbered the wealthy in a big way, and as had happened in Russia, we could have overthrown the elite. The answer was tied up in the TOC H boys…religion! It not only teaches men to love each other, but also to love one's enemies. Here's the genius of it for the elite; if you get this right, then after you die, you'll be in heaven. If you get it wrong, however, you'll burn in hell. So your life on earth might be shit, but be a good boy, put up with it without complaining, and all will be OK when you die. You couldn't invent a better 'keep them in their places' system if you tried!

It wasn't long after joining the party that I discovered that the British authorities were very suspicious of us and kept a close eye on all we did. It was crucial that we didn't make our move until we could be sure of our success, and this meant that we had to work closely with the Soviets. I visited Moscow in 1932 and was blown away by the city and the way the Party ran it. The place was ordered, and everyone we met was alert and positive about their lives. There was such a confident air of purpose. All the religious texts had been burnt, along with any historical accounts that suggested a splendid past. Now, at last, human beings could create their own future and set out towards it—it was brilliant! Science had put God out of a job by filling the gaps in our knowledge that, up to now, our ancestors could only explain by referral to a deity. Not only that, but once we had managed to liberate the working classes around the world by getting rid of the elite, we would then be able to dispense of private ownership. All this would mean that everyone would get an equal share—no-one starving and no-one getting wealthy at the expense of others. Simply applying common sense showed that the option to share everything was the best way for a society to live.

It was around this time that a rival dream of the future emerged in Germany. Adolf Hitler began to speak of an empire that would be dominated by a small number of ethnically pure Northern Europeans. Whilst Communism was all about equality, National Socialism pursued the principle of evolution by natural selection. Nietzsche had argued that the human race would never progress if successful humans shared with the unsuccessful. Instead, they ought to have courage and take advantage of their superiority for their own benefit. If that was tough on the weak, then that's natural selection! Whilst I could see there was a sick logic to it, it went completely against the grain. I threw in my lot with Communism and hated Hitler and his cronies.

Shortly after returning home, the people in Moscow asked me to sever my links to the Communist Party, and instead, begin to embrace a middle class lifestyle. They wanted me to behave as though I had been disaffected by my time in Moscow, and seduced away from my first principles by mounting material prosperity. This was fairly straightforward because I had a good job, and I actually enjoyed living this lie. I had been contentedly married, to Shirley, since 1923, and Alice, our only child, was able to go to a prestigious girls' boarding school. Since this was part of my cover, the Soviets paid her fees. My wife, completely unaware of all this, enjoyed her privileged lifestyle, and I prospered at work. In some ways, it was an outrageous double life that I found myself living—I was pretending to be everything that I railed against—but it never really felt odd. The two conflicting lives somehow sat comfortably beside each other.

When Britain declared war on Germany in 1939, therefore, I found myself in a place I could only have dreamed of. I had followed my father into his firm and was involved in the design of aircraft. As a result, two key aspects of my life were in place. First, I was involved in the effort to rid the world of Adolf Hitler and his fascists. Secondly, I had access to information that my people in Moscow were keen to get their hands on. I was contributing to the preparations for the second phase of the liberation of the World's underclasses, even as I was working to defeat Hitler. Having dealt the Third Reich a knockout blow, there would follow the elimination of the Western elites, including, of course, the British ruling classes.

Maybe the end of the war meant that MI5 had more resources to focus on dealings with the Soviet Union, who knows, but at one of my regular drops with my contact from the Soviet Embassy in March 1951, I was taken off in a car to the Sussex coast. There, a boat was waiting to ferry me out to a large fish factory ship standing off in the Channel. My cover had been blown. The last thing the KGB wanted was for me to be taken and for the British to discover the extent of the information I had passed on to them.

It's now six months later and everything has completely unravelled.

I'm totally disillusioned. This is not just a passing emotion, but rather the result of discovering that everything that I have believed in has turned out to be false, and worse than false, downright wicked.

Imagine if the Archbishop of Canterbury was shown a skeleton with cast iron proof that it was that of Jesus Christ. Whilst his faith would be shattered, at least he would have the compensation of knowing his life had focused on being nice to other people. In the Great War, I had mown down men, just like me, because the King and his cronies had persuaded me, a naive eighteen year old, that this was a noble thing to do. Since the 30's, I've been passing on British military secrets and betraying people to the Soviets. I was in the grip of another monstrous lie spread by a different set of individuals. Having killed the Tsar, far from liberating the working man, they had simply taken over all the privileges that the Tsar and his crew had enjoyed. Even

Moscow couldn't hide the extent of Stalin's purges in the 1930's, and today, individuals disappearing off the streets is an accepted fact of life. If the Tsars had been dismissive of their serfs, at least they had never terrorised them in the way that the Communist Party does. Yes, I had accepted that blood would inevitably have to be shed in order to liberate the working man, but I've discovered that not only is the blood-letting still going on, but that the working man is just as likely to be a victim.

There's more, however. There are special shops for Communist Party officials that sell desirable Western goods no-one else can buy. This is the supreme irony of a movement that aims to get rid of all privilege. They've built luxury holiday dachas on the Black Sea coast that welcome them in the Summer, and, most in your face of all, middle lanes down the main thoroughfares in Moscow that provide unimpeded rapid journeys for their chauffeur driven Zils. And yet, they insist that all are equal and everyone is to be called 'Comrade'. It's complete bollocks!

Worst of all, Shirley and Alice are not joining me. It's not just that their lives in England are good—my daughter read medicine at Edinburgh University and is now a paediatrician—but they had no inkling of my clandestine life. I can only imagine the sense of betrayal my wife feels at having discovered the truth of my life, and anyway, how could I even begin to explain what I've discovered since arriving here.

As I look out over the Moscow skyline, I see the latest, and greatest of Stalin's *Seven Sisters*—Moscow State University. Built as a Skyscraper to rival those in New York, it is massively imposing and an eloquent testimony to man's search for knowledge. It powerfully represents, in glass and concrete, the unshakeable permanence of human reason as the source of all truth. It's where the truth of everything is being unearthed. All those thousands of windows, far from letting the daylight in, are there to radiate out the light of human achievement.

Who are they trying to fool?

I've been lied to twice over. First, it was King and country that did for me, and now, I've been gullible enough to believe that the Communist leaders might have been different.

I'm lost.

I look back to the folly of the Great War, and my patriotic zeal, and whilst I remain grateful that my faith in the past was laid to rest, I replaced it with a monster. I had believed that man was now smart enough to plot a future that would at last sort things out. Science had supposedly brought an end to the influence of ancient superstition over man's actions, and we should now logically work out the best way for all to live. Hitler had decided that this was all about self interest and persuaded the Germans that they were the superior race. On the other hand, Communism had at least believed in the equality of all people. However, in exterminating those who refused to accept this principle, they ultimately turned out no better than Hitler. Equality, fantastic in theory, is in fact pure fantasy.

So my problem is not simply the past, it is the future as well.

Up to now, I've always had something that I was not just prepared to sacrifice myself for, but was also willing to kill for. Initially, it was the past glory of the Empire, and latterly, it was the future glory of the Communist dream. Now, there's nothing. I no longer trust anything anyone says to me, especially those in authority. I find myself isolated, trying to make sense of a life that has no purpose. I've become marooned in a world of my own making, and I'm struggling work it out. If the primary goal in life, forged into my soul in the bloody days of 1918, and doggedly pursued ever since, has proven to be unattainable... well, what's the point of keeping on trying to walk on water after you've discovered it can never be done?

The past means nothing to me. Technically, I'm an Englishman living in Moscow, but any sense of being English was finally put to bed when I betrayed my neighbours to the Communists. And, when the future ceased to be of any relevance, I found myself trapped in the present, and realised I'd lost the two people who made my present worth living. As I searched frantically for a fresh truth, I reflected on the relationship my parents enjoyed, and the strength they showed when they rejected the war at its outbreak. What was the truth of their relationship? I thought of my marriage and the truth of my double life that had for so long lain at its heart. I thought I could keep it under wraps but it caught up with me. Here is a truth that was real enough to wreck my life. Having concluded that there was no truth to be derived from the past, and that the truth of the future was vain, I'm now confronted by the very opposite. I'm here because of the truth of past events, and the impact of my decisions. Moreover, I'm miserable because the truth of my future is all too plain to see.

And these facts are taunting me.

So here I sit at my table in the cocktail bar of the *Hotel Intourist*, just off Moscow's Red Square—a privilege accorded to me having been made a 'Hero of the Soviet Union'. I'm sipping Scottish malt from cut Romanian crystal and scrutinising some drawings. The Soviets are taking advantage of my training, and

I'm working on a bomb that takes out airfields. It will be a sort of pod slung under a fighter bomber flying beneath radar cover that scatters different types of munitions as it passes over thc runway. Small bomblets will pockmark the runway with craters, some of which have delayed fuses so that craters continue to be made. There are also loads of small anti-personnel mines that will maim the ground crew. But I'm working on a really clever mine designed to kill the driver of the bulldozer that is clearing away the rubble. When the bulldozer blade strikes the mine, it tilts towards the blade and fires off a shaped charge that pierces the blade and smashes into the driver. As I study the drawings, I'm deep in thought. I'm trying to focus on the moment when I realise I'm tapping the palm of my left hand against the side of the table with a rhythm and a force that has emerged from deep within my soul…tap tap tap tap tap.

"There are no facts, simply interpretations"

— Friedrich Nietzsche —

One Last Story

"No inherent moral or ethical laws exist, nor are there any absolute guiding principles for human society. The Universe cares nothing for us and we have no ultimate meaning in life."

— William Provine —

Getting on for a hundred years ago, Millicent Haddock married Herbert Dickson. Given that he was the butcher's delivery boy, and she the daughter of the house he was delivering to, the match didn't go down too well. Millicent and Herbert were singularly undeterred. They got married and went into production, so to speak, and ended up with seven children. Bert, as he was known, was a loner. But, if he was painfully shy in public, he was a bully at home. That he himself was badly bullied by his father, and on one occasion almost drowned in a water butt, perhaps offers some kind of explanation—though not an excuse. Millicent, or Miggie, looked after her brood, picked up the pieces, and was a brilliant mother. The family struggled, but Miggie proved to be very adept at making ends meet and squirrelling away money so she could spend it on the children. Altogether, this was a thoroughly unremarkable family living a tough life in Stockport either side of World War Two.

And then Bert's father died.

A young curate called Bernard, who looked after the corrugated iron mission chapel on the estate, took the funeral. Bert was deeply impressed. In fact, he was so impressed that he became a Christian, and decided that the Dickson family would start going to church. At first, Miggie was very cynical about her husband's conversion. Over time, however, Bert's character mellowed. Whilst he was still prone to making arbitrary decisions that served no purpose other than to establish his authority over his children, Miggie was impressed enough to decide to follow Jesus as well. She recalled, before her death, an incident that was to have such a far reaching impact that, at the time, she couldn't possibly have foreseen it.

She was attending a mid-week women's prayer meeting, and all the other women were describing what they wanted to give to Jesus. Miggie kept quiet because she felt she had nothing to offer—her time was completely taken up looking after her family, and there was certainly no spare cash knocking around. On the way home, feeling depressed, she suddenly had a thought…a brainwave…a divine prompt! She realised that she did have something special to give to God, namely her seven children. As she continued on her way, this is what she did. Whilst one might find it fascinating that she didn't share this information with her family till shortly before her death, it is nevertheless a fact that each of her seven children grew up to follow Jesus in a very committed way. Three of her four sons would become Christian ministers, and one of her daughters would marry one. God was clearly delighted with her gift!

Barry was her second son and the first to be ordained. He met Margaret Philip when he was a law undergraduate at Liverpool University, and it is clear that had he not been a Christian, Margaret would never have considered him. In fact, Barry emulated his father in that Margaret came from a large house in Birkenhead that housed a respected Merseyside family. Margaret's mother was vehemently opposed to the wedding, her daughter being way too good for this working class man, and, although to no avail, she did her utmost to prevent it. They married, and in due course brought into being three brand new people, of which Christopher was the second.

And so we bump into Christopher, the subject of this, our final story. He is by this stage well into the second half of his life and coming to the end of an intense period in which he has been earnestly asking himself the BIG questions of life. Whilst he always wanted to think that he was his own man, that his life was no-one else's business, and that his identity could be what he chose it to be, he now increasingly sees that none of the above is the case. He never chose to exist; life was given to him, as indeed was his body. Whilst he might be able to choose different courses of action and to develop himself in different ways, he remains restricted by those aspects of him that are given. He will never, for example, be a composer of orchestral pieces. Unlike Mozart, who was composing whilst still in nappies, he struggles even to remember the notes of the infernal *chopsticks* tune that all the kids used to play on the piano in the church hall. Neither will he ever be a ballet dancer; his physique is all wrong, and his sense of rhythm badly flawed.

But, he is a contented bloke.

As the white hairs in his beard gradually become more prominent, he finds himself increasingly relaxed in his own skin, and at ease with himself—who he is, how he was made, and ultimately, who and what he has become. His experiences tell him that you discover yourself through your relationships, both with others and with your Creator. And, the times when things go badly pear-shaped can be the most fruitful in terms of self-discovery.

So, you now know that Christopher Dickson exists, but what of his beliefs and experiences in life that have brought him to this enviable place?

Christopher was created by Christian parents and raised in a vicarage in the West Riding of Yorkshire. As he grew, it never even occurred to him that there might not be a God, nor that what he was taught at Sunday School, and at Christian house parties, was anything other than the truth. It wasn't until he entered his teen years that the teaching he was receiving began to clash with the life he wanted to lead. The church youth group he attended happened to be a very large one, and it was well led. They were taught what constituted a Christian lifestyle and frankly, it didn't appeal to him. In fact, he was by this stage into all kinds of things that were forbidden to young Christians. He just got on with it, as many teenagers do, and lived a double life. The size of the youth group meant that quite a few of its members were at school with him, and, like him, they were cheerfully leading this double life. It was at this point that Christopher first realised his particular way of looking at things, one that would come to heavily influence his life choices.

Christopher tends to observe the actions of other people and judge them—who doesn't? But, for him, this is a very practical undertaking. If there is something that makes someone look sad in his eyes, then he works very hard to avoid doing the same. He found himself at school with other teenage boys who were enthusiastically studying the Bible on Sunday, but then on Monday, quite openly behaving in ways proscribed by the youth leaders. There was one boy in particular who simply got under his skin, and he was definitely not going to be like him, no way! So Christopher had a choice…and he chose a path that allowed him to do as he wished. He decided that God didn't exist. There were, after all, plenty of people around who thought this, and God was completely absent from everything he was taught at school. There was also, he suspects in hindsight, more than a hint of rebellion against his upbringing. As with the sons and daughters of many vicars, he decided to cast off religious restraint.

Irrespective of whether this approach works for other rebellious vicarage kids, it was a disaster for Christopher. He was singularly unsuccessful at being rebellious. Stuff he wanted to do never came his way, and he had a niggling conscience that held him back from some of the excesses that were going on around him. In the end, all he achieved was to become a rather sad social disaster with very few friends, in fact perhaps only one. The latter years of his schooling were simply a waiting game… waiting to get out and into the Navy—an ambition that could trace its roots back to a time that he could barely remember. Ability, rather than work, got him through his O levels. If his A level results then revealed that such an approach doesn't continue to be effective, he nevertheless scraped the two he needed to get into the Britannia Royal Naval College in Dartmouth.

Leaving home offered him an opportunity to start again. School had been miserable, and he wanted to be someone else.

Christopher was in a new place and was known to no-one—here was his opportunity. As an emphatic act of will, he renamed himself Kit. Amazingly, Kit found that he was 'one of the boys' and that people actually sought out his company. Socially, this was amazing, but sadly, his attitude to work didn't change. He missed deadlines, disastrously left preparation to the last minute, and regularly underperformed. Meanwhile, he poured Ushers bitter beer down his neck in alarming quantities, so whilst Kit was the life and soul of the Floaters[1], he was a failing Midshipman. He did pass out of Dartmouth eighteen months later, but he did so on Captain's Warning. His time in the Fleet was equally pathetic, and drink did it for him in Bordeaux. That, as far as the Navy was concerned, was that. Kit's Captain applied for, and was granted, permission to have him 'withdrawn from training'.

Over time, as Christopher reflected on his years in the Navy, a number of particular episodes lodged themselves in his mind—those that exposed the confusion he now realises he was living through. One evening, the Floaters was packed and Dave, the landlord, was understaffed and so asked if Kit would help out behind the bar. He was dead chuffed to be asked, but, later that evening, he nicked some cash from the safe that sat open just inside the kitchen—he was badly overdrawn. The money sat in a neat pile, and he only took the top couple of notes. Whilst Dave never challenged him about it, neither did he ever ask him to help out again. But, Kit had just stolen from a friend. He did the same on the eve of the Easter Ball. His stiff-fronted shirt was

1. The Floating Bridge Hotel

crap—he hadn't laundered it since the last ball. So, he nicked one belonging to his mate, Simon. Slipping into the Chief's office, he grabbed the key to Simon's cabin, and took it. In spite of all this, Kit remained a popular person and so never saw what was coming to him. One final episode, in retrospect, said it all. About a month before Bordeaux, Nick, a fellow member of the ship's wardroom—and one Kit really looked up to—asked if he wanted to go out for a drink. Once again, he was dead chuffed. They drank and chatted, and that, as far as Kit was concerned, was that. Except of course, it wasn't. What he was daft enough not to realise was that Nick was giving him wise and friendly advice, telling him that he was a good person, but that he was on the brink of throwing it all away. It was only after Nick had learned of Kit's ultimate fate that he pointed out that the time ashore had in fact been a deliberate effort to save a Naval career.

So…

Christopher remembers arriving home, unannounced, with all his gear and telling his astonished parents that he'd decided to leave the Navy. It wasn't for him; he wanted to try something else. They were shocked because, up to that point, all they had heard from him were the glowing reports of a burgeoning career, one that included being the Colour Officer for the Dartmouth Passing Out Parade. People at home were surprised to see him around, and were asking why he was no longer in the Navy. It wasn't long before Kit realised he just had to get out of it. Whilst applying for the Hong Kong Police Force, he came across a small ad in The Times seeking crew to complete a yacht's journey from Gran Canaria to Cape Town. He responded and to his amazement and delight, was taken on. For a variety of reasons, it was at times both exciting and scary, but two life changing events occurred during the passage.

First, the ageing yacht stopped off at the Cape Verde Islands for a week in order to decide whether she was capable of making the passage. The decision was made that she was, but, during that time, Kit had done the stuff that had got him kicked out of the Navy.

Secondly, the four people on board had to stand three hour watches through the night because the autopilot didn't work and the yacht had to be constantly helmed. These watches were done alone, and a couple of nights into the Atlantic, Kit had gotten to thinking. If being kicked out of the Navy hadn't taught him anything, then getting drunk in the Cape Verdes made him sit up and take note. He had sometimes pondered the morality of some of his actions, and had tended to dismiss any conscience pangs as a legacy of his vicarage upbringing. After all, his very decision to become an Atheist had been predicated on his desire to create his own moral framework. But now, as a crisp wind blew into his face, moral contemplation felt utterly irrelevant. Whether drunken evenings were, of themselves, right or wrong, was a side issue; what was more pressing were their very real consequences. That, and the fact this behaviour that had ended his Naval career was continuing unabated.

And then he realised that with the ending of his Naval career came a chronic loss of purpose. He was running away from his past, but the very fact that he was in a small yacht in a vast ocean seemed to emphasise the fact that he was lost. You're in the Navy, you have a career, orders to carry out, qualifications to gain, promotions to pursue. What did he have to aim for now?

He looked from the tiller to the compass and realised that both were of little use without the other. Not only that, but he was a rubbish helmsman who had just lost his compass.

It was blindingly obvious that he had to do something radical if he was to rescue himself. Running away hadn't changed anything.

The wardroom on board ship had been a lively environment, and Kit had been in the company of some top blokes, several of whom he really admired. But, as he reflected, he found himself trying to judge how many of them were content with life at that deeper, more profound level. As the yacht steadily progressed Westwards, propelled by a persistent Southerly trade wind, he struggled to recognise even those officers he looked up to as being deep down content. The First Lieutenant was one such character, but even he didn't convince Kit that he had found that level of inner peace. As he pondered this, he realised that the people he did know who had this contentment were all people who he knew from his Dad's church back home.

Nowadays, Christopher occasionally reads the diary he wrote during that trans-Atlantic passage, and, when he does so, he notes that on Sunday, February 7th, 1982, he recorded his decision to ask Jesus to forgive him. This brief sentence is backed up by an admission of having an aimless life, together with the observation that the happy people he knew were all Christians. This deep stuff is then followed by a comment about the flying fish that were landing on the deck each night!

Kit had been in charge of his life since his decision to do away with God, but having achieved his childhood ambition, he had, unbelievably, thrown it away. Not only that, but deep down, he was ashamed of much of what he had done, and it wasn't that he'd failed to learn the lessons—it was way more scary than that. Kit had learned the lessons, but had found himself incapable of acting on them. Out of sheer desperation, he decided that he would try following Jesus, and behave as though God did exist on the grounds that God couldn't make a worse job of his life than he had. For six months, he would consciously live as a Christian, but, over that time, God would have to show him he was relevant to every aspect of his life. Kit was not interested in a Sunday-only religion; he was looking for a way of life that would extract him from the hole he had so comprehensively dug himself into.

Christopher can't recall feeling any different upon saying the prayer asking for forgiveness, and he's not sure he gained very much from reading the New Testament that, unbeknownst to him, his father had snuck into his bag as he left home. The yacht sailed into English Harbour and Christopher remains proud to this day of his part in ensuring that they hit Antigua spot on after a 28 day passage with nothing to guide them save a watch, a nylon sextant, a nautical almanac, and a compass. That night, Kit got drunk, got into a fight with the yacht's owner, and jumped ship. Had anything changed? His faith was certainly fragile, and his diary reveals that during the voyage, he still regularly wondered whether God did in fact exist. But, he had made a commitment and he was determined to stick with it.

The next morning, he had rung home to inform his parents that the boat had made it to dry land, and, along the way, he told his mother he'd become a Christian. She gave him the contact details of some Christian friends they knew in Miami because

Kit had decided to head to the States for a bit of travelling. It is interesting to recount that later, she told him that when he rang, the phone system at home had been out of order. They were waiting for the telephone engineer to attend to it. She had been walking out of the kitchen past the phone and had heard it softly click and so had picked it up to see why. It was Kit…the coincidences had just begun!

Anyway, God's 'welcome home' present was four months in Syracuse, NY, with Uncle Jeremy, one of his dad's younger brothers who was a minister of a church in that city. God knew what he was doing.

When Kit ditched God, he remembered taunting his youth group leader with a photo of himself. He had said that this was a photo of his god, and that he prayed to him all the time—he always answered the prayers either with a 'yes', a 'no', or a 'wait'. (They had been taught that this was God's way of answering prayers and it had always struck Kit as being pretty pathetic, since whatever happened, one could always say that God had answered your prayer.) When Kit was in Syracuse, he discovered that God did answer prayers in ways that regularly beggared belief. The coincidences mounted up to a point where, as far as he was concerned, the word 'coincidence' finally had to be abandoned in favour of 'answer'. When Christopher looks back on his sojourn in the States, he increasingly recognises the importance of those days. They established a foundation for his faith that was rich in experiences.

Another change took place in that he reverted to being Christopher once again. In a weird way, his temporary use of the diminutive has allowed him to park the disaster that was his time in the Navy on the grounds that it belongs to another existence altogether.

Christopher is the kind of person who instinctively applies his reason to life's ups and downs, its big questions and its trivial aspects. He's a thinker who loves convoluted arguments and the manner in which reason can unlock all manner of conundrums. He gets a real buzz when he fathoms something out, and there is not much that matches his sense of achievement when he finally decides he understands something. Not only that, but he enjoys the challenge of trying to explain complex matters to others in a way that doesn't belittle the issue but instead makes it accessible.

It is therefore perhaps a little surprising that the times when he finds himself most questioning his faith is when he's listening to a reasoned debate between Christian and Atheist apologists. If Christopher is reading one of their tomes, then he's ok with the output of the Atheists—the likes of Richard Dawkins and Sam Harris—because he can comfortably unpick their arguments. On the other hand, if he's reading Christian authors like John Lennox or Alister McGrath, he finds himself pretending to be an Atheist and wondering whether he's being persuaded…and often he sees gaps in their trains of thought.

So, whilst reason is pivotal to Christopher as he work things through, it is, on its own, incapable of giving him solid assurance that his decision to follow Jesus was a wise one. This is not to say that his faith is unreasonable. Given who he is, it *has* to be reasonable, and following Jesus Christ has to stand up to his ability to reason things through. On the other hand, those who believe there is no God can also marshal a case that is not, on the face of it, unreasonable. So it is that he has to supplement his reason with his experiences. When reason fails him, Christopher can turn to a lifetime of experiences that are both personal and compelling. For example:

When one of Christopher's daughters was six weeks old, he and his wife noticed during nappy changing that she wasn't straightening one of her legs. It just so happened that a GP friend was visiting, so they asked him to take a look at it. As there was some swelling, he suggested that she should be taken to the hospital. Two hours later, she was in the operating theatre with three consultants working on her. If the diagnosis was grim, the prognosis was appalling. This tiny little person had osteomyelitis in one of her femurs. The consultant orthopaedic surgeon had never seen it in one so young, and so advanced was it that he reckoned it had set in whilst she was still in the womb. The x-rays showed a hole in the bottom of the bone, rather like one you might spot in a decaying tooth, and the knee joint also had septic arthritis. She would recover, but the growth pad at the base of her femur was wrecked—the bone would lose 60% of its growth. Her knee joint had been damaged beyond repair, and it would need to be locked at a beneficial angle when she was maybe twelve years old.

Christopher didn't pray. He couldn't pray. It was impossible to believe there could be a God who could allow his tiny, vulnerable, innocent little baby daughter to suffer in this way. Unlike his teenage decision not to believe, this failure in faith was spontaneous and terrifyingly out of his control. It also had major implications, since Christopher had not long since been ordained a priest in the Church of England. Needless to say that loads of people were praying, but he was not. Two things resulted.

As the months passed, the various specialists became increasingly surprised by the fact that the femur was growing at the same rate as its opposite number. As well as this, the knee was functioning freely. Without the scar from the operation, one would have no idea that anything had happened in the first place. So, had the consultants got it wrong…or had God answered some prayers?

But well before that, in fact the Sunday following her admission to hospital, Christopher had found himself in the company of 400 young people at a youth service in a Baptist Church on Shooters Hill. Everyone was singing with gusto accompanied by an energetic worship band. He stood there, hands thrust in pockets, unable to join in. This was just the pits in terms of how he was feeling, and he would have given anything to be anywhere but in that place.

And then it had happened.

He couldn't describe it in terms other than that, all of a sudden, he knew absolutely for certain that God was, God is, and that God loved him and his daughter. Whatever happened, it'd be ok. Feeling all fuzzy and light-headed, he found himself quite literally singing his heart out. He praised God in the words of a song that perfectly expressed the overwhelming joy, and relief, that he was feeling at that moment. An experience like this cruises way beyond the bounds of reason, but so what…life is to be experienced as well as analysed.

Sometimes, when Christopher *analyses* all this, he's struck by the modern imperative to do precisely that, to analyse in detail life's experiences, one's reactions to them, one's thoughts, and one's actions. There is the temptation to believe that herein lies the key to mastering oneself and one's destiny. For sure, there are plenty of people out there who will suggest that this is the case, and even, for a fee, offer to accompany you on this journey of 'self discovery'. On the other hand, Christopher has discovered that the matter of one's identity, ironically, is not to be unwrapped by becoming a self-obsessed navel gazer. We are, all of us, pretty complex creatures. Nonetheless, he is learning to live with the person he is discovering himself to be through his relationships with both his fellow human beings and his Lord Jesus. In fact, he is beginning to like himself—nay, even to love himself!

This latter development has been one of the most startling, for although the second Great Commandment given by Jesus demands that one loves one's neighbour *as oneself*, Christopher has always found it easier to concentrate on the former and ignore the latter. Somehow, the latter always felt kind of selfish. But, one day, reviewing his priorities in life with a good friend, he came to what he refers to as his *Air-safety Brief* moment. The steward on the plane always advises that, in the unlikely event of the plane's cabin depressurising, oxygen masks will drop down in front of one's face. The instructions are insistent; namely that you must put your own mask on before attempting to help anyone else with theirs. If who and what you are is a gift from the Creator, *and* if he loves his creation, it is not unreasonable to suggest that one does likewise. Furthermore, to look after and nurture oneself is to make it way more likely that you'll be in a position to love others effectively.

And so, as this One Last Story draws to its conclusion, let me say, if you haven't already guessed, that we have left fiction behind. What you have read, barring the necessary obfuscating name changes, is a potted account of my life to date, as I remember it.

I was 'Bob' in the Navy, and the one or two colleagues I've intermittently kept up with still call me Bob—I kind of like it that they do. Whilst there is so much of that time that I want to forget, I can't help but reflect on the wisdom of Adrian Plass, who said the shit you sometimes find yourself up to your neck in, is in fact the principle ingredient of manure, that universal agent of growth.

Where am I now? Amazingly relaxed in spite of having only a part-time job in a shop, and monthly monetary outgoings that exceed monthly incomings! Jesus told me the other day that I needed to be patient, for there is 'power in the waiting'. Whilst some might call me deluded, my experience tells me otherwise, so I'm waiting patiently. You may well have heard of the 'swimming duck' analogy that people have, in the past, trotted out. Whilst their progress might appear to be calm and serene on the surface, they are, beneath the surface, frantically flapping like the swimming feet of a duck. By and large, I'm the opposite. I might, on the surface, be all over the place, and believe me, at times, I am. However, beneath the surface, I am rooted in the love of God and just know that in the end, all will be fine. I know where I've come from—I've been called by God—and so I know where I'm headed. This releases me to live in the present, enjoying the challenges but not beating myself up when I get it wrong. Yes, Christianity makes complete sense to me at a rational level, even to the point where science, in as much as it is able to do so, bolsters my beliefs. But, just as important to me are the fifty five years that I have lived on this planet, and my life experiences that have brought me to this moment as I sit here on the 1115 Virgin East Coast Express travelling from Leeds to London Kings Cross.

I am reminded of the Children of Israel at the end of their 40 year journey through the Wilderness. At times, their faith has faded and even evaporated altogether and God, understandably, gets frustrated. If one reads the accounts though, one discovers that through his prophets, God calls his people to cast their minds back in order to recall his gracious hand on their lives. At the end of the book of Joshua, the people have at last crossed the Jordan and entered the Promised Land. Joshua gathers them together and offers them the ultimate choice. They can, if they wish, serve the gods of the land they have entered, the gods worshipped by the current occupiers who are more sophisticated than they are, more prosperous, and more secure behind their city walls. Alternatively, they can stick with the God who brought them out of slavery in Egypt and to the land they are now standing on. The future that God is offering is based on his promises and not on present realities. On the other hand, the gods of the land appear to blessing the current inhabitants with a desirable lifestyle—one that 40 years in the Wilderness have doubtlessly left the Israelites desperate for. Joshua simply says, "Choose you this day whom you will serve.".

But, like Sonja Kharoud, I find in this offer a challenge…I live in a consumer society where, supposedly, the consumer is sovereign. I am governed by a parliament that is intent on offering me choices on the assumption that this will appeal to me precisely because, when I make a choice, I exercise my sovereignty. So, am I a Christian simply because I prefer its 'offer' to that of Hinduism or Zoroastrianism? The notion of choosing which supreme authority is right for you is profoundly ludicrous. By definition, there can be but one supreme authority, and the idea that one may select one's 'God' simply conceals the fact that ultimate authority rests with you, not the deity. This is why, though it embarrasses me when I say it, I am a follower of Jesus Christ because he chose me. The accounts we have of Jesus' ministry reveal an individual who, whilst he accepts the worship of others, never demands it. Instead of saying 'worship me', he says 'follow me'.

So, therefore, what of my decision to follow? I sense that without overpowering my freewill, God nevertheless gave me the resolve to make the decision to follow, and the strength to persevere. Not only that, but God's Holy Spirit seems to inform my reason, and over time, I increasingly see things as I think he wishes me to see them. Indeed, as I look for a purpose, something that will bring meaning to my *three score years and ten*, then I look to Jesus' distillation of the divine imperative: To love God, and to love my neighbour as I love myself.

At this level, it is so simple—to love God is to obey God[2]—but once you begin to burrow into this adage, you encounter a sophistication that does way more than simply welcome you in. Step across its threshold, and be introduced to a radical understanding of life and its meaning. As you explore this fresh life through prayerful study and action, a couple of things happen. To start with, you begin to realise how much it all makes sense, and you feel yourself beginning to gain wisdom. Then, as time passes, it dawns on you that even a lifetime of exploration

---

2. See 1 John 4:7-5:5

will never exhaust the wisdom of God. God's wisdom is infinitely more complete than either you or I are able to comprehend. It is indeed as St Augustine wrote "We are talking about God. What wonder is it that you do not understand? If you do understand, then it is not God."[3]

God and Love. This was what Sonja was mulling over on the bench overlooking Windermere. Love, by its very God-given definition, cannot be forced out of someone—it can only be received from someone who freely gives it. It is the benchmark by which all relationships are to be measured, and it wraps together reason and experience in an inseparable bond. There can be no more profoundly positive experience in life than that generated by being on the receiving end of unconditional love. The decision to love, however, has a rational component that must be able to overcome the emotion of the moment. By this, I mean that, on occasion I have felt less than loving towards another person. But, by and large, my reason has held sway and prevented me from acting in an unloving manner that I would have deeply regretted. To love someone requires, not infrequently, a cold determination to put that person first. Jesus absolutely did not want to be crucified—as his struggle in the Garden on the night of his arrest shows—but somewhere deep within his soul, he found the resolve to overcome his emotion and he submitted, out of love, to his father's wishes. It is not surprising, therefore, that the Apostle John, in one of his letters to a group of young followers of Jesus, makes one of the most profound statements of all time, that…

---

3. St Augustine, Sermon 117.5

"God is Love, and those who live in Love, live in God, and God lives in them."

"No inherent moral or ethical laws exist, nor are there any absolute guiding principles for human society. The Universe cares nothing for us and we have no ultimate meaning in life."

— William Provine —

29694479R00123

Printed in Great Britain
by Amazon